Moonlight on the Lido Deck

A Standalone Novel

Sail Away Series

Book Six

Violet Howe

FOR JOHN

Thanks for being my favorite cruise partner

Books by Violet Howe

(Continued on next page)

Visit www.violethowe.com to subscribe to Violet's monthly newsletter for news on upcoming releases, events, sales, and other tidbits.

Moonlight on the Lido Deck

By Violet Howe

PROLOGUE

I f Katie had known what a bad day it was going to be, she might have stayed in bed with the covers pulled over her head.

Instead, she'd leapt from the bed in a mad dash as soon as she realized her alarm hadn't gone off. She wondered later if that had been some kind of omen, or if perhaps it was the universe's unsuccessful attempt to prevent the day ahead.

She'd spilled coffee down the front of her shirt on her way to work, and it was only after she'd gotten in the elevator to head up to her office that she realized she was wearing two completely different black pumps.

"Where have you been?" Mandy asked from the desk next to hers as Katie set down her purse and what remained of her coffee. "Terrance is looking for you."

"What?" She glanced at her watch and frowned. She'd counted on his typical late arrival to cover her own. "He's never in this early."

Mandy stood and came closer, leaning in to whisper. "Something's going on. He and Rochelle have been behind closed doors in the conference room all morning with some guy I've never seen before. Carol over in Acquisitions said she has it from a solid source that it has something to do with the merger."

Trepidation churned in Katie's stomach, causing the bagel she'd wolfed down on her brisk walk to work to feel like a big rock in her gut. "Should I be worried? They said in that last meeting they didn't expect any layoffs, right?"

"That's what they said." Mandy chewed on her bottom lip as she glanced over her shoulder in the direction of the conference room. "Maybe it's good news. Maybe they're going to transfer you to a different department, and you won't have to work for Terrance anymore. Or maybe you're getting promoted! Are you wearing two different shoes?"

"Yeah." Katie looked down at her feet and sighed. "It's a new fashion statement I'm making."

"It's a brave one," Mandy said with a grin.

Katie smoothed her hand over her hair, wishing she'd taken the time to do something more than the loose knot she'd twisted it in. "Should I go find Terrance or wait for him to come and find me?"

"I told him you'd gone down to the mail room, so he said to send you to the conference room when you got back."

Her trepidation had grown into a nauseating sense of dread. "Thanks for the cover. I guess I'll get it over with. No sense standing here keeping us both in suspense."

"Wait." Mandy grabbed the black sweater from the back of her desk chair. "Put this on. Maybe it will hide that other fashion statement you've got going on—you know, the coffee stain?"

"Oh. Thanks. I forgot about that."

Terrance called for her to come in on the first knock,

and she swallowed hard against her fear as she entered the conference room. The unfamiliar man in the suit sat at the other end of the table, barely giving her a glance as he stared at the papers spread across the table in front of him.

Rochelle, the office's human resource manager, was seated to his right, and the troubled expression on her face as she looked up at Katie and then immediately away did nothing to ease Katie's fears. Mandy was right. Something was going on, and it was serious.

It was the look Terrance gave her, though, that tanked any remaining hope that she'd merely been summoned to help with their unknown project. Her boss's usual scowl had softened into a frown, and his eyes were clouded with what appeared to be pity or regret, neither of which were emotions Katie had ever seen him display.

'Katie, there you are. Have a seat, please." Terrance stood and pulled out a chair for her at the end of the table nearest the door, several seats away from the three of them.

Her palms had become sweaty with apprehension, and she rubbed them on her skirt before clasping her hands in her lap.

The man in the suit introduced himself, and then in a voice much too cheerful for his message, he explained the reasons behind the company's recent merger and detailed how the downturn of the economy and the shifting landscape of publishing had led the new management team to make difficult decisions. Decisions no one wanted to make.

The reasons behind the decisions and management's feelings regarding them didn't change the outcome for Katie. She'd only been with the company for six years, the lowest seniority in her department, and therefore, she would be one of the few layoffs that had been deemed necessary.

She tried to listen as Rochelle went over the terms of the severance package they were offering, and she was fairly certain she'd managed to nod when a response was expected. The signature she scrawled at the bottom of the papers Rochelle slid across the desk looked nothing like her usual signature, but in the end it didn't matter. Less than two hours after she'd arrived late to work, she was headed back home in a dazed state of shock, her feet shuffling along the sidewalk as her mind reeled.

She hadn't particularly liked her job, and there'd been many days when she'd wanted to hand Terrance her notice and tell him to find someone else to terrorize. But it was one thing to quit on your own terms and quite another to be told you were no longer needed.

Laid off. Let go. Cut.

Unemployed.

She couldn't believe it. She'd been working at one job or another since high school, even juggling two different part-time positions while she was in college.

How was she going to pay her bills if she couldn't find a job before the severance ran out? How would she find another job in publishing when the entire industry seemed to be cutting staff rather than adding them?

It stung that the decision was based only on the length of time she'd been on the job and not on her performance. Yes, there were people who had been with the company longer than she had, but she was a hard worker. Even Terrance had called her a real go-getter. She'd lasted longer under his supervision than any assistant he'd ever had, and she'd taken great pride in knowing she did her job well. But none of that mattered. It was a numbers game, and her number was up.

Never had she felt so tossed aside. So unappreciated. So adrift.

She blinked back tears as she forced herself to keep putting one foot in front the other on her way back to the apartment. She considered calling her mom, but news of her lay-off was sure to send her mother into a worry spiral, which meant Katie would end up comforting her mother and reassuring her that everything would be okay instead of the other way around.

She could call her sister, but Maya's idea of commiseration was to point out the bright side in any bad news. Katie's wounds were too fresh and too raw to deal with Maya's boundless optimism and annoying pep talks. She needed to drown in her own misery a bit before she could even think about trying to climb out of it.

Grant would be the best one to talk to. He wouldn't offer her any comforting platitudes. He'd just agree with her that it sucked without making a big deal of it, which was what she thought she needed most. But even with the five-hour time difference between New York and London, it was early enough in the day that he would still be at work, and he didn't like for her to call during his office hours.

Surely, under the circumstances he wouldn't mind, though. What boyfriend wouldn't want to comfort his girlfriend when she'd just lost her job?

Back when he'd first taken the position in London a little over a year ago, they'd talked multiple times daily, and he had welcomed her call at any time.

But as he grew more engrossed in his role there, he'd grown increasingly irritated with any interruption while he was working. Then, one day he'd simply announced that he would prefer for her to only contact him after his workday was done. Even that proved problematic with the time difference though, since he would be out and about doing evening activities while she was still at her desk, making any in-depth conversation pretty much impossible on either end.

Eventually, they'd settled into their current routine of one daily phone call as soon as Katie got home from work in the US while Grant got ready for bed in the UK, and then on Sundays when they could both set aside time to be home and available at the same time, they'd do a video chat.

It wasn't ideal for maintaining a relationship, but on the few occasions Katie had protested, Grant had reminded her they'd known it would be difficult when he accepted the two-year London assignment. Each time, Katie had backed down and agreed, again, that the short-term sacrifice was worth it for Grant's career and thereby, their long-term future. But on days like today when she just needed to talk to her boyfriend, it felt like he was on another planet instead of another continent.

The doorman for her apartment building scrunched his brows in confusion when he saw her coming up the steps.

"Ms. Torrey? Back so soon?" He held the door open and attempted to take the box she held. "Let me get that for you."

"I got it, Rex." She carried the cardboard against her chest like a shield, unwilling to hand over all the personal belongings she'd accumulated in her desk over the past six years.

"Is everything all right?"

"Yep. Fine, thanks." On a typical day, she'd engage in

conversation with Rex, but this wasn't a typical day, and she didn't have it in her to make small talk.

He seemed to sense that, and much to her relief, he remained silent as he accompanied her to the elevator and pushed the button for her.

"Ms. Torrey?" called a voice behind her.

She turned with a frown as the new building manager walked toward her at a brisk pace.

"I'm so glad I caught you," he said. "Could I speak with you for a minute?"

Katie had held it together as she packed her desk and said goodbye to her co-workers, and she'd managed to mostly keep the tears at bay on the walk back to the apartment. But the closer she got to home, the nearer she was to having an emotional meltdown, and the last thing she wanted was a witness.

"Can it wait, Mr. Paxton? I'm not feeling well at the moment."

It was his turn to frown. "I see. I'm sorry to hear that. Well, how about I ride up with you and we can chat in the elevator?"

She didn't have the energy to argue with him, so she just stepped inside the elevator and waited while Rex held the doors for Mr. Paxton to enter. With a nod and a sympathetic smile in her direction, Rex pushed the button for her floor and then exited the elevator before it closed.

"I wanted to speak with you regarding the lease," Mr. Paxton said once the doors had shut. "I wasn't certain how you intended to handle things moving forward, and I wanted to make sure you knew you'd need to fill out an application and submit your financial documentation if you intend to renew once this lease term is up."

Blinking slowly in bewilderment, she tried to make sense of his words.

"Um, I'm not sure what you mean. We checked before I moved in, and we were told that according to the New York Roommate Law, I don't have to be added to the lease to live with Grant."

"That's correct, but Mr. Whitman is no longer using the apartment as his primary residence since he is residing outside the country."

"Right, but it's still his apartment. Other than the clothing he took with him, all his belongings are here. It's his residence, and I'm just a roommate who pays half the rent. The London job is a temporary assignment, and once it ends, Grant will be moving back in here."

"That's not what Mr. Whitman indicated to me in my conversation with him earlier today. The lease is up for renewal in sixty days, and today was the deadline to give notice of intent. Since Mr. Whitman said he does not intend to renew, you'll need to fill out an application and be approved to carry the lease on your own if you plan to stay. Typically, we would go to our waiting list to fill a vacancy, but as you are already living in the apartment, we're willing to make an exception."

The elevators doors opened, but Katie remained glued in place as her dazed brain struggled to catch up. "What are you talking about? What do you mean he doesn't intend to renew? You must have misunderstood. He has nine more months in London, and then he'll be back."

The doors began to shut, but Paxton held his arm out to block them.

"Oh, dear. I fear I may have let the cat out of the bag. My apologies, Ms. Torrey. I assumed Mr. Whitman would have told you before he told me. I would encourage you to speak with him as to his intentions, and then come and see me. I'm sure we can work something out."

The elevator began to buzz its dissatisfaction at being held so long, and Katie stepped off as his words replayed in her head.

Grant didn't intend to renew the lease?

No. It had to be a misunderstanding. Paxton was new. He'd gotten something wrong. She'd speak to Grant and have him talk to Paxton and clear things up.

She dialed Grant's cell number as soon as she'd gotten inside the apartment and set the box from the office on the floor. It no longer mattered if it was work hours or not. She was certain Grant would agree this was important enough to warrant an interruption.

The call went to voice mail, so she texted him that it was an emergency and asked him to call her back right away.

Her phone rang almost immediately.

"I'm about to go into a meeting," he said without any greeting. "Is this truly urgent, or can it wait?"

"Yes, it's urgent. That new manager, Paxton...he said you told him you're not renewing the lease and that I have to fill out an application if I want to stay here. I need you to contact him and straighten this out, Grant. I've had the worst day already, and I can't deal with this on top of everything else."

"You've got to be kidding me. I can't believe that guy."

"Yeah, I know, right?" Katie plopped down on the couch, relieved to hear Grant's voice, even if he was irritated.

"I'm sorry, Kate. I intended to talk to you about this on Sunday when we could speak face to face, or, um, on video, at least. I never dreamed he'd say anything to you before I had a chance to explain. I told him we needed some time to sort things through."

For the second time that day, Katie felt like a dull-bladed knife had been twisted into her insides.

"Sort what through? Am I going to have to put my name on the lease since you're not technically living here? I can't get approved for a place like this, Grant! Even if I still had my salary, it never would have been enough, and now that I've been let go, I don't have any income to show them for qualifying."

"What do you mean you've been let go?"

This was not how she'd intended to tell him. "I got laid off today. They're cutting staff due to the merger, and I'm the lowest in seniority in my department."

"Christ, Kate. This is horrible timing. I've got to get in there and get set up for this meeting. I'm doing a presentation for the executive board. I don't need this right now."

The emotions she'd been battling for the past couple of hours were too close to the surface to keep down any longer, and his clipped attitude towards her coupled with his indifference to her distress pushed her over the edge.

"Well, gee, Grant. I'm so sorry that I didn't get terminated at a more convenient time for you and that the possibility that I'm going to be homeless isn't more pressing than your meeting."

"You're not going to be homeless. Don't be dramatic."

"I'm not being dramatic," she said in a voice that was very much dramatic, but she didn't have it in her to care at the moment. "Can you just call Paxton after your meeting and tell him this is still your primary residence?"

He groaned and released a soft swear. "I can't get into this right now. Can we please wait and talk on Sunday?"

"What is there to get into? I can't afford this place on

my own, with or without my job. If they're going to make us put the lease in my name, then we have a problem. You have to tell them you're coming back."

"That's just it. That's what I was planning to tell you. I'm not coming back, Kate. I like it here. I want to stay here. They've offered me a long-term role, and I've accepted it."

"What? Just like that? We're not even going to discuss it? I mean, that's great that you're happy, and it's awesome that they've offered you a role, but I can't believe you just took the job without even telling me. How on earth are we going to make this work? Am I able to get some kind of visa so I can get a job over there? And what about my family? I know your parents can afford to travel and visit you, but mine can't. My mom will freak out if I tell her I'm moving to London. I already know what Maya is going to say. She'll swear this is the silver lining to me getting laid off, and maybe it is since I can join you sooner, but—"

"Kate, I've met someone. I'm sorry. I never meant to hurt you, and I never meant to tell you like this, but...this relationship hasn't been working for either of us for quite some time. We've both needed to move on, and maybe a clean break is the best way to do it."

The air left her lungs and she couldn't pull any in to replace it. Her vision began to go black around the edges as she sat staring at the wall. "What?"

"Look, this is not how I planned to do this. Again, I'm sorry. But I can't be late for this meeting. I'll call you when I get off, and we can discuss this further. It's gonna be fine, though. I've been thinking about this quite a bit, and I think once you get your head wrapped around it, you'll see this is for the best. We can talk more later, but right now, I have to go."

She couldn't reply. She couldn't think. She couldn't process.

"Kate, I don't want to hang up on you, but I must go. Please say something so I can end the call."

"Screw you." She tossed the phone onto the coffee table and then lay curled up on her side as the tears began to flow. This time she didn't even try to hold them back. The dam broke, and sobs overtook her as she processed the double whammy of two enormous losses at once.

She didn't know how long she lay there or how long it took for her tears to stop flowing, but it was dark outside when she finally sat up and looked toward the window.

The world felt like the bottom had fallen out and everything had gone black. Desperate for any hope to cling to, Katie called the one person she knew would be able to find a ray of light in the darkness.

"I know this must seem like the end of the world right now," Maya said once Katie told her all that had happened. "But I think we have to look on the bright side."

"If anyone can find one, it'll be you." Katie chuckled through her tears. "You've got your work cut out for you, though. How are you going to spin a positive to me losing my job, my boyfriend, and my apartment all in one day?"

"Easy. You're better off without all three, and you never would have left them all behind if your hand wasn't forced. I'm not saying you don't have every right to be upset, but let's be realistic here. You hated working for Terrance, and the job wasn't what you'd hoped it would be."

"True, but as long as I was working for a publisher, I

had a foot in the door for when I get around to writing my novel."

"But with the hours you were working and the amount of stress you were under, you never seemed to find the time and energy to write anything at all. Now maybe you'll be able to. You still have all the contacts you made when you were there. Why not look at that severance package like it was an advance on your book? They're giving you, what, twelve weeks? That's three months for you to buckle down and write. Then, when you're ready to pitch it, call up your old co-workers and have them slide it onto the right desk."

"I can't just take off work the next three months and do nothing but write. I have to find another job. And another place to live." Another muffled sob escaped Katie as she looked around at the home she'd soon have to leave. "I really loved this apartment. I won't ever be able to afford anything like it on my own. I probably won't even be able to find anything in this neighborhood. And no matter where I go, how can I get approved for a lease without a job?"

"Okay, I'm not even going to pretend it doesn't suck to lose that apartment. You're right. It's great. Location, layout, furnishings, view. The whole thing. But do you know how many times you've told me in the past year that you miss Florida? That you hate the weather in New York?"

"That's just during the winter. I hate the cold. The ice. The snow."

"What about how expensive everything is?"

Katie wandered over to the window and gazed out at the lights of the city. "Florida's expensive, too."

"Not as expensive as living in the city," Maya said with a scoffing laugh. "Your severance pay would go a lot farther if you had less going out for the next three months. Why don't you come back home and live rent-free? For a while, anyway. That way you could spend more time focusing on writing and less time worrying about finding a job and a place to live."

"Oh, I don't think I could do that. Move back in with Mom and Dad? No, thank you. I'd rather eat ramen noodles and live someplace the size of a closet."

"No, silly. I'm not saying you should move back home-home. Move back home to Florida and stay with me for a while. I've got an extra bedroom. I just need to clean out my art supplies and come up with a bed from somewhere. Which I can totally do."

The thought of living a block from the beach was tempting. It would be a nice change of scenery, and for a moment, Katie let herself imagine a daily routine of sitting in a chair with her toes in the sand and her laptop open. Maybe without the stress she'd been under the past few years, she'd finally be able to get words on the page again.

But then, reality came crashing in like a huge wave, crumbling the dreamy vision.

"I wouldn't do that to you," she said with a sigh. "I don't wanna crowd your space and be a burden."

"Are you kidding me? I'd love to have you. And hey, as far as being a burden, I could always use help in the surf shop." Suddenly, Maya gasped. "Katie—that's it! That's the silver lining."

"What is?" Katie asked, confused as to what Maya meant but hopeful it would be good once she understood it.

"My friend Ben invited me to go on a cruise with him and his family next month. I figured I'd have to close the shop to go, but if you come here and learn the ropes, you could run the shop for me while I'm gone."

Katie's thin thread of hope unraveled. "You're saying the silver lining to my life falling to pieces is that I get to work for you in the surf shop while you go on vacation?"

"It's a silver lining for both of us! I get to go on the cruise without having to close the shop, yes. But in return, I'll provide you with a place to live rent-free and stress-free so you can write the next Great American Novel and become a bestselling author. Then, you can move back to New York in your own penthouse apartment and you won't need someone like Grant to sign for it."

Katie was silent for a moment as she mulled it over. Working for her sister and bunking in her guest room wasn't a scenario she would have willingly quit her job and moved back to Florida for, but since she was currently unemployed and about to be homeless, the offer seemed at least somewhat attractive. It wasn't like she had a better alternative.

How bad could it be to spend a couple of months living at the beach, helping her sister run the tiny surf shop, saving as much money as she could, and maybe finding time to finally finish her novel in the meantime?

ONE

It took less than a week for Katie to get all her belongings packed to take Maya up on her offer. The apartment had been fully furnished with Grant's things when she moved in, so she only had her clothing, her toiletries, her books, and the few personal mementos she'd either brought from home or acquired during her six years in the city.

The meager number of boxes only reinforced the feeling that her grand New York adventure had been a big, fat failure.

She'd arrived in the Big Apple right after college graduation, ready to leave the small-town version of herself behind to forge her own metropolitan path—a path she was certain would lead to travel, culture, broader horizons, lofty achievements, and maybe even romance. Back then, she'd been ready to conquer the world.

Now, she was going back to Florida with nothing to show for her efforts. No job, no published novel, and no partner. Sure, she'd been exposed to a bit of culture, but she'd only gotten one passport stamp—for a long weekend visiting Grant in London after he first moved there. A weekend they'd spent holed up in his flat due to the nasty stomach bug he'd contracted the day before she arrived.

And though Maya seemed excited for her to come, Katie found it hard to match her sister's enthusiasm. She was grateful to have a place to go—and relieved she wouldn't have to move back to Cedar Creek to live with her parents—but she never dreamed she'd come to a point in life where she needed to move in with her free-spirited sister and work at the surf shop.

It was temporary, of course, but that didn't make it any less humbling.

Who would have ever thought the sister voted "Most Likely to be a CEO" in high school would end up dependent on the one voted "Most Likely to Live in a Bohemian Compound"?

Katie had always been the more studious of the two, a lifelong high achiever who usually spent every free moment with her nose in a book and excelled at anything remotely academic.

Maya, on the other hand, had loathed school and its inherent pressure to conform. Though she was freakishly adept at anything athletic, Maya had been most passionate about art. Well, art and anything that would push the tight boundaries set forth by their parents.

Bill and Rosalyn were on good terms with their oldest daughter now that she was an adult, but teenage Maya's wild nature had gotten her into all sorts of trouble, culminating in her being kicked out of the house when she quit high school in her senior year, three months shy of graduation.

Watching her parents struggle with her older sister had made Katie even more determined to succeed and make them proud.

But now she'd failed at that, too.

Her mother had been near hysterical since Katie broke the news about the lay-off, break-up, and temporary arrangement with Maya.

"I still can't believe this is happening," Rosalyn said when Katie called to check on her. "I haven't been able to eat a thing. Haven't slept a wink. This is just awful. Terrible."

"It'll be okay," Katie reassured her mom, hoping she was right. "It'll be fine."

"No, it won't be! Not with you leaving New York. And to work in your sister's surf shop, of all things! You didn't get a college degree to work in a surf shop, Kathryn. You were destined for greater things than that. It's not too late to change your mind, you know. Grant said you could stay there until the end of the month."

"I don't want to stay here, Mom. Everywhere I look, I see something that reminds me of him. It's *his* apartment. *His* furniture. *His* dishes. *His* towels. I have to get out of here."

"Surely, you have a friend who'd let you stay with them until you find another job. There are plenty of publishers in New York who would just jump at the chance to hire someone with your experience. Did you ask your boss if he'll write you a letter of recommendation?"

"No. I didn't." She bit down on her lip as she weighed whether to tell her mother the truth, and then she drew in a deep breath and confessed on the exhale. "I'm not so sure I want to be in publishing anymore."

"What? Why on earth not? You've always wanted to work in publishing."

"No, Mom. I've always wanted to be a writer. You and

Dad convinced me that getting a job at a publisher might be a way to get my foot in the door."

"Well, it still can be. Being a writer is a treacherous career path. You know that. It's inconsistent and uncertain. There's no guarantee you'll ever have a paycheck. Publishing puts you in the same industry but with much more stability."

"That might have been true in the past, but things have changed drastically in the past few years. There's a lot of upheaval and instability in publishing right now. It's not the guaranteed paycheck you think it is, and I didn't really enjoy it, to tell the truth. As much as I hate that I got let go, I'm not upset that I won't be doing that job anymore. I never told you how stressful it was because I didn't want to worry you."

"I couldn't get much more worried than I am right now," Rosalyn said with a huff. "You can't just give up. You've worked so hard to get to where you are."

"That's just it though. I haven't gotten anywhere. At all! Everything I've done, all the work I've done, it's been for nothing. I have nothing to show for it. In my career or my personal life."

"Oh, honey. You've just hit a rough spot, that's all. You'll find another job, and you'll meet someone else. Someone just as successful as Grant."

Great! Katie thought. *Someone else who will put their career first. No thanks!*

As she ended the call, she knew there was no way to convince her mother this was the right choice. She wasn't even convinced herself. All she knew was that she could no longer stay in New York and be bombarded with reminders of what might have been.

No. What she needed most right now was an escape. A

chance to catch her breath and find a bit of peace before making any decisions about the future.

The future. What future?

For her entire life, Katie had been working toward one achievement or another. Make good grades in middle school to be placed well in classes for high school. *Check.* Make good grades in high school, be in all the right clubs, and hold all the right leadership positions to be accepted by the best college. *Check.* Maintain a high GPA at the university and do all the right internships to ensure a good candidacy for the right job. *Check.* Nail the interview, get the job, move to the city. *Check.* The successful boyfriend her mother could be proud of. *Check.* The loft apartment in the trendy neighborhood. *Check.*

Check.

Check.

Check.

She'd checked all the right boxes, but she'd still ended up lonely and miserable.

Maybe it was time to scrap all the plans and think outside all the boxes.

"I was going to paint over the flowers and the lime green, but I wasn't sure what you'd like," Maya said as she led Katie into the small bedroom at the end of the hall. "I figured we could just go to the paint store and pick something out now that you're here. Whatever color would make you happy. Multiple colors, if you'd like."

Katie set her suitcase beside the narrow twin bed and stared at the huge flower blossoms painted in every color imaginable across the nearly-fluorescent green walls. It was a far cry from the calming, neutral tones of the sunlight-filled loft apartment she'd left that morning, but that apartment —*that life*—was no longer hers. She winced at the thought but managed a smile for Maya.

"It's fine. It's...bright. Cheerful. I...um...thanks again, Maya." She shoved her hands in the back pockets of her jeans as she turned to her sister. "I really appreciate you letting me stay here."

"Of course. Anytime. I appreciate you helping me out so I can go on the cruise."

"Right. The cruise. Who's this guy you're going with?"

"Ben. I'm pretty sure you met him when you came down for the weekend that time. Tall, dark, handsome, a little broody, but funny as hell, and a heart of gold."

"Um, no. I'm pretty sure I'd remember meeting someone that like."

"Hmm. Maybe. Maybe not. I'm almost positive Ben was part of the group that went with us to that concert on the beach."

"Could be. Who knows? You introduced me to so many people that weekend that I couldn't keep them all straight. You have, like, a kajillion friends. Besides, that was a while back. It was right after Grant moved to London, so it was over a year ago."

"True." Maya turned to pull open the top drawer of the dresser in the corner, which had been painted hot pink. "I emptied this out so you can put your clothes in it, and I cleared out some space in the closet if you need to hang anything."

"Thanks," Katie said as she lifted the suitcase onto the bed and unzipped it. "So, what's the story with Ben, and why are you going on vacation with him?"

"We've been friends a while. I originally met Ben through Louise."

"Ugh. Louise who shattered your heart into a million pieces?"

"Yep. That's the one. Ben's an artist too, so he and Louise ran in the same circles. They did a show together at a local gallery, and we all went out afterwards. Ben and I just...clicked. We hit it off. We became fast buds, and then, when Louise and I broke up, Ben was really there for me. I feel like the rest of that group kind of went with Louise because they knew her first, and that's how things go when there's a nasty break-up. But not Ben." Maya crossed her arms with a sigh as she leaned against the door frame. "He stuck by me, and he refused to let me lay in bed all day with the covers over my head. He made me get out. Forced me to eat something every now and then. Kept me from drinking myself silly. And we've been tight ever since. He's exactly what I imagine it would be like to have a cool older brother. I mean, he's only six months older than me, but he's one of those guys who just seems wiser than his years, ya know?"

Katie laid her folded shirts in the dresser drawer. "You said it's a cruise with his family? How'd you get roped into that? You're not exactly one who enjoys family time."

"I'm fine with other people's families. Just not ours! But I figure I owe him one, so this is my way of helping him out."

"By going on a cruise? How's that helping him?"

"He's the only one of his siblings who's not attached, which evidently drives his mother nuts. They're doing this trip for his nephew's birthday, and his mother put a lot of pressure on Ben when she found out he was planning to come alone. She threatened to bring his ex-girlfriend, which he wasn't okay with at all."

"Wow. And I thought our mom was overbearing."

"Our mom *is* overbearing! Ben says his mom never got over him breaking up with his high school girlfriend and moving away from their hometown. I guess she's always hoped he'd move back there someday to marry that girl and work at his father's law firm."

"I thought you said he was an artist," Katie said as she grabbed a hanger from the closet.

"He is, but he got his law degree before he worked up the nerve to tell his family he wasn't going to follow in his father's footsteps. Anyway, you know I love a cruise, and I'm always ready to travel, so I volunteered to go and be his girlfriend for the week."

Katie paused in hanging up the dress and turned back to stare at her sister.

"But...you're...gay."

"Well, I don't plan to have to sex with the man, Kate. We're just telling his family I'm his girlfriend. I don't think they'll come into our room for evidence."

"You're sharing a room with him?" Katie asked, unable to hide the surprise in her voice.

"Yes. I'm sharing a room with him. A room with two beds. What's the big deal?"

Katie shrugged. "Uh, there's not one, I guess. I just can't imagine going on a trip with somebody and pretending to be in a relationship with them. I mean, don't you think his family will notice that you guys aren't...you know...*together*? I mean, they don't to have to come into your room to realize that you guys aren't, well, affectionate with each other."

Although, even as she said the words, she realized she and Grant had never been affectionate in front of anyone.

And that she'd never met his family in all the time they'd been together.

Maya plopped down on the bed and tucked her feet underneath her. "I don't think we'll see them a whole lot, honestly. Ben said we'll do our own thing for shore excursions during the day, and then we'll meet up with the family at dinner and probably go our separate ways afterward. It's not like they expect us to make out during the meal. And give me some kudos for my time spent in community theater, would ya? I can play the role of Ben's girlfriend convincingly for a week. I've already come up with my character's backstory and motivation. Wanna hear it?"

"No, but I have no doubt you can pull it off. I'd never be able to do something like that."

"Sure, you could. You were a great little actress back in your theater days."

"It's not acting. It's lying."

"Ah, that's right. Being dishonest has never been your strong suit."

"You say that like it's a negative quality."

"Not at all. Your honesty is something I admire. I know I can always count on you telling me the truth." She cocked her head to the side and pulled a sweater from the suitcase. "You realize you aren't going to need this in Florida, right? This is too thick for even the coldest day we have."

"I know. I just threw that in the suitcase because I'd already boxed up the rest of my sweaters when I saw it hanging by the apartment door. Most of my wardrobe is not going to cut it in this heat and humidity, but it's not like I can just go buy a bunch of new clothes when I don't have a job and I don't know how long I'll be here."

"Don't worry. I have plenty of stuff you can borrow."

"Really? Wow! You never let me borrow your clothes when we were in school."

"Yeah, well, I'd like to think we've both grown up a lot since then. Hey, a bunch of my friends are heading over to the Riverfront Park amphitheater to listen to a band that's playing. There'll be food trucks, maybe some craft vendors, and it's cool music. Could be a good time. You interested?"

"No." Katie shook her head, thinking the last thing she wanted was to be surrounded by a bunch of festive people enjoying their lives. "I'm pretty beat so I'll probably turn in early. You go ahead, though. I don't want you to miss it."

"Are you kidding me? It's your first night in town. I'm not leaving you here alone to sulk. If you don't want to do the concert, fine, but you need to get out and breathe in the fresh salt air. You hungry?"

Katie hadn't had much of an appetite since everything had fallen apart, but at the mention of food, her stomach rumbled. "I could eat."

"Great, because I'm starving." Maya slapped her hands on the tops of her thighs and then stood. "Why don't you change into something more beach-appropriate, and we'll head over to the Salty Crab and grab something to eat."

At first, Katie was skeptical that a little salt air and some seafood could make her feel better, but it was hard to stay down around Maya's upbeat outlook, and by the time they'd finished dinner, Katie already felt lighter.

"Are you up for a little detour?" Maya asked on their way home from the restaurant.

"What kind of detour?" Katie raised a wary brow, worried her sister would want to go out when all she wanted to do was climb into bed.

Maya's grin widened. "I've got something I want to show you. I had planned to wait until tomorrow, but I'm too excited. I wanna show you now! It won't take long. It's only a couple of blocks from here."

"It's not a club or a bar, is it? I'm not in the mood for a crowd."

"Are you ever in the mood for a crowd?" Maya teased.

"No. But I can psyche myself up for it when I have to. Tonight, I'm too tired to even try. I just want to crawl in bed."

"No crowd. Just me and you. Give me a few more minutes, and then I'll get you home to bed, *Grandma*."

"Okay, but what are we doing?"

"You'll see! It's a surprise. I can't tell you until we're there."

In only a few minutes, Maya had pulled the car into a parking space in front of a vacant building.

"What's this?" Katie asked, staring at the windows for any clue, but they had been covered with paper from the inside.

"C'mon. I'll show you."

To Katie's surprise, Maya grabbed a set of keys from the car's console and used them to open the door to the building, flipping on the lights as she led Katie inside.

"Welcome to the new and expanded location for Seahorse Surf!"

"What? This is yours?"

"Yep," Maya giggled as she twirled in a circle with her arms spread wide. "Isn't it awesome?"

"It's huge!" Katie turned in slow circles, staring at the large open area with a wall of windows fronting the street. It was easily three times the size of Maya's current store.

"Yeah, it is. I've been cramped in the other building for a while, and I can't continue to grow the way I want to if I stay there. This will allow me to increase my inventory and start carrying a wider variety of merchandise. More clothing. Jewelry, sandals, bikes. Whatever I want."

"Wow. That...sounds...awesome. Really." Katie nodded, biting down on her lip. "It's gonna be great, and I'm fully on board in supporting you."

Maya lifted a brow. "Why do I have a feeling you're about to say something that sounds like Mom or Dad?"

"Ugh. You're right. I was about to say something that sounds like Mom or Dad."

"Then chances are, I don't want to hear it."

"I know, and the last thing I want to do is rain on your parade, but are you sure about this? It's a lot of space, Maya. It's a huge commitment. In time. In energy. In money. Lots of money. Do you really need something so...big?"

"I know that look on your face. That look says you think I'm being *crazy Maya*, running off to chase some impulsive idea without thinking it through."

"That's not what I'm saying. I just don't want you to bite off more than you can chew. How are you going to afford this?" She held her hand and looked away. "You don't have to answer that. It's none of my business, and you're an intelligent woman, and I'm sure you've done the math." She scrunched her face like she was straining with the effort to be quiet, and then she looked back at Maya and repeated the question. "Seriously, how are you going to afford this? The rent alone must be a fortune, and you're talking about tripling your inventory to fill this kind of space. And it's great that you're looking at bringing in new merchandise, but that's risky. You already know what sells where you're at now. You've done really well there."

"You're right. I have. Which means there's no reason to think I can't be just as successful here. You get so passionate about the negative outcome. Why can't you direct that kind of energy into focusing on the positive outcome?"

"Because you're my sister, and I'm worried. I don't want you to do this all alone and end up with regrets."

Maya walked over to Katie and gave her a hug. "Thanks, baby sister. I appreciate your concern, but it's okay. Really. I'm not doing this alone, though. I have a very generous benefactor who wanted to invest in real estate in this area. Sort of a silent partner, I guess you could say. One with attorneys and accountants and people who know how to protect both our interests and make sure we're starting off on solid ground. So, this isn't some crazy impulse. It's been well-researched, well-planned, and carefully laid out. And it will work."

"I'm sure it will," Katie said. "Like I said before, you've been successful in your endeavor so far, and I'm sorry the first thing I did was express doubt. I really am happy for you, and I'm certain you'll make this the best surf shop ever."

"C'mon. Let me show you the rest of the place.

She led Katie through the back of the store, where the changing rooms were being built. Through the door at the rear of the building, they entered a hallway, and Maya smiled as she pointed toward doors on the other side of the hall.

"Restrooms are over there. That one's a storage room, but it's kind of small, so I've been talking with the contractor about maybe knocking down that wall and incorporating the other end of the hall to make a bigger room." Maya opened the next door for Katie to peek inside. "This was a conference room, which I don't need. I'm thinking down the road I may convert it into a yoga studio and start offering classes. That last door is for the office, which I could probably use for more storage if I have to. What do you think?"

"I think you're insane. But I've always thought that. As far as the building goes, it's great. It's gonna be awesome. I love you, and I am behind you. One hundred percent."

"Thanks." Maya took Katie's hand and squeezed it. "That means a lot to me. I haven't told anyone else—you know, meaning Mom or Dad. And I probably won't until I've got it all up and running. I want to stay surrounded by positive energy so everything goes smoothly in the building phase. But I wanted you to know. Especially since you're here with me to see it happen. For a little while, anyway."

"I'm excited to see it come to fruition, and I'll help out however I can while I'm here."

"Good. I'm glad to hear that. I was thinking that once you feel comfortable being in the surf shop alone, maybe you can cover that for me so I can be over here more. My business partner's been out of town for an extended period, and it would be great if I could be here to oversee the renovations in person instead of over the phone."

Once Maya had finished showing Katie around, they headed back to Maya's bungalow to turn in for the night.

Even though Katie was tired from the day's activities, she felt more hopeful and more optimistic than she had since the day she was laid off. Maybe even for months before.

It was partly due to Maya's unwavering optimism. It was impossible to spend time with her sister and not feel lighter and more positive about the world. Maya's enthusiasm for life was contagious, and Katie had forgotten how easy it was to feel good in Maya's company.

But it wasn't just Maya's mood rubbing off on her.

For the first time in her adulthood—maybe for the first time ever—Katie felt free. She had no responsibilities. No goals. No plans beyond helping Maya until she got back from the cruise. And after that? Who knew what was to come.

The uncertainty and the not knowing were both exhilarating and terrifying. While it was unsettling to feel so untethered from her own life, it also made her feel like the future was wide open. Like she could choose anything, go anywhere, do whatever she wanted.

For as long as she could remember, there had always been a goal she was striving for. A hurdle to cross. A challenge to overcome. A next step to reach.

Now, with all that stripped away, she felt like the ticking clock in her head had gone silent.

Maybe it was the silence that lulled her to sleep, and maybe it was the blanket of security and love her sister's house offered, but whatever it was, it worked. Katie slept soundly through the night, despite the sag in the little bed, the glow of the green walls around her, and the droning voice coming through the wall from Maya's bedtime meditation soundtrack.

Two

By the end of Katie's second week back in Florida, she and Maya had settled into a routine that offered a much gentler pace than she'd had in New York.

In the morning, she'd sit and watch the sun and the seagulls as Maya surfed, and then they'd do a yoga routine together on the beach. Back at the bungalow, Maya would whip up a smoothie or an egg-white omelet for the two of them, and then they'd head to the surf shop, where Katie took meticulous notes on all she would need to know to run the shop in Maya's absence.

Then, once they closed the shop for the day, they'd head over to check out the progress at the new building. The more details Maya shared about the project, the more excited Katie became, and she looked forward to seeing the changes in the space each day.

Evenings involved either dinner somewhere near the water so they could hear the waves coming in, or Maya would cook something for the two of them and then they'd go and walk along the shore.

Katie slowly began to relax.

The past few years had been non-stop stress with long hours and never-ending demands at work and a lonely dissatisfaction at home. Breakfast had consisted of a muffin or a granola bar on the run. Terrance frowned upon anyone taking a lunch break, so she'd grab something from the vending machine and eat it at her desk. Dinner always ended up being a frozen meal or takeout she picked up on the way home, where she'd collapse on the sofa exhausted. Her only escape had been reading, which she stayed up much too late doing, resulting in a rushed, tired morning as the cycle repeated itself over and over again.

In comparison, life with Maya seemed like a vacation, and though Katie was nervous about managing the store alone during Maya's cruise, she couldn't help but notice how much calmer she felt. How much more at peace she was, even after such a short period of time.

Still, uncertainty about the future was ever-present in her mind, and there were times—usually after she got off the phone with her mom—that the worry threatened to consume her.

"You can't let her get to you," Maya said after Katie had finished a particularly difficult conversation with their mother.

"She's right though." Katie sighed as she swept the construction dust from the floor in the new building. "I have no plan beyond the next month when you return from your cruise. I haven't sent out a single resume. I haven't even looked at a job listing. It's like I've just stuck my head in the sand and disengaged from reality."

"It's been two weeks!" Maya said as she carried a ladder over to where the paper in the window was beginning to fall. "It's fine to just take some time off, Kate. You've got money coming in from the severance package and your bills are minimal, so it's not like you're on the verge of being destitute. And I know working for me isn't your dream job or your long-term solution, but you can stay here as long as you want. Until you decide what's next, anyway."

"And what if I have no idea what comes next? What if everything I thought I wanted suddenly doesn't make sense anymore, and I don't know what I want to be now that I'm all grown up?"

"Then, you don't make any decisions until you know." She positioned the ladder under the window and shoved her fist through the roll of tape so it encircled her arm like a bracelet, leaving her hand free to hold onto the ladder as she climbed. "Don't obsess over the future so much. That fearful energy blocks the possibilities the universe is trying to send you. You need to learn to be in the moment and find the good in where you're at. Be present. Be grateful. Then, once you take the pressure off, you'll find it easier to figure out what you want to do next."

"That's so easy for you to say. You've always lived that way. I haven't! My entire life has been spent focusing on what comes next. When I was in middle school, I was focused on high school. When I was in high school, I was worried about college. Since college, I've been trying to move up at work and worrying about what would happen when Grant came back. I don't know how to be in the present, Maya. I've always lived for what tomorrow would bring, and now tomorrow is completely unclear, and I don't know what to live for."

"Live for you! That's it. It's that simple. Do what makes you happy. Do what makes you feel good. Have you felt good the last six years? Have you been happy? Because it sure didn't seem like it from here."

"You don't understand." Katie shook her head in frustration and bent to hold the dustpan while she swept the pile into it. "We're wired differently, okay? We always have been."

"Maybe so, but being happy is a choice anyone can make." Maya stretched as far as she could, leaning precariously over the side of the ladder to secure the corner of the paper to the wall. "You have to choose it every day, though. Sometimes every hour. And it can be all around you, but you won't know it if you spend all your time chasing some future version of what you think being happy should be."

Katie stood upright and put her hand on her hip. "Some of us like to have a plan in place, okay? We can't all live with our heads in the clouds trying to channel the right energy like we're on a perpetual vacation."

"That's what you think of my life?" Maya turned to look back at her sister as she climbed back down the ladder, but in her distracted state, she missed the bottom step. Her foot hit the ground at an awkward angle, rolling her ankle to the side beneath the force of impact. Collapsing to her knees with a cry of pain, she rolled to her side, clutching the injured foot.

"Maya!" Katie yelled, tossing the broom aside as she rushed to her sister's side. "Are you okay?"

Maya sucked in a sharp breath with another yelp of pain. "I think my ankle might be broken," she gritted out through clenched teeth. "Maybe my foot, too."

"What can I do?" Katie knelt beside Maya. "We have to get you to a hospital. Should I call an ambulance?"

"No. I'm not dying. You can drive my car. My keys are in my pocket."

"How will we get you to the car, though? You shouldn't put any weight on it. And I haven't driven a car in years. We should just call—"

"I'm not calling an ambulance and pulling them away from life-threatening emergencies for a broken ankle. Now, for the love of God, Kate, please just help me get to the car and then get me to a hospital before I pass out from the pain."

"Two months," Maya said with a groan as they waited for her to be discharged from the hospital. "I can't believe I'm not allowed to put any weight on my foot for two whole months. No surfing. No running. No dancing. Two months! They can't be serious."

Katie frowned with a lifted brow. "You broke your ankle in two places and had to have a pin put in it. That's pretty serious. Did you honestly think you'd be back to running right away?"

"No, but when I broke my foot before while I was skateboarding, they just put me in a boot and had me use crutches for a week."

"That was a contusion, which you reinjured, plus the addition of what the doctor said was a very nasty break in your ankle. Much more serious."

"This will put me so far behind with the renovations." Maya sighed, shaking her head in frustration and disbelief. "And there goes my cruise."

"The cruise is still two weeks away," Katie offered, trying to be the optimistic one but feeling woefully unqualified. She was usually the one receiving the pep talk, not giving it. "The doctor said the next few days recovering from the surgery will be the most painful, so you should feel much better by your sail date. And you've got this handy-dandy knee scooter to get around with. I think it'll be easier than crutches."

Maya laid her hand on her forehead and closed her eyes. "I can't go on a cruise with my foot in a boot and my knee propped on that stupid cart. I'd be in everyone's way, blocking traffic and slowing everything down. No. No way. I have to tell Ben I can't go."

"Maybe you could get a wheelchair and use that on the ship."

Maya opened her eyes and shot Katie a glare. "No. All of our excursions involved some kind of physical activity, which I won't be able to do now. And knowing Ben and the type of guy he is, he'd insist on staying behind with me, so then he'd miss out, too. No. It'd be better if I didn't go at all. At least then, he has a chance to have fun."

It was unsettling to see the always-upbeat Maya in such a negative state. Katie felt desperate to try and pull her sister out of it, but she had no idea what to do.

"Hey! What would you tell me if the situation was reversed? You'd say I had to stay positive. That I need to look for the bright side. There's got to be a bright side in this somewhere, right? You always say—"

"The bright side is this happened before we left and not on the ship." Maya closed her eyes again as she massaged her temples. "It is what it is. I need to tell Ben I can't go. I promised him I'd be there for him, and now I have to let him down."

"I'm sure he'll understand, but maybe it won't come to that. Let's see how the next couple of days go. You're probably going to be a whiz on that scooter in no time. Maybe it won't be so bad."

"You know, Kate," she said, opening her eyes to level another glare at Katie, "contrary to popular belief in this family, my head isn't always in the clouds. I've got to deal with reality like everyone else, and right now, the reality is I have to cancel this cruise."

Guilt shot through Katie as she replayed their conversation from earlier, and she wished she could take back what she'd said just before Maya fell.

"I'm sorry, okay? I never should have said that. I wish I could approach life the way you do. No, really, I do. You're a helluva lot happier than I am, and more successful too. And yeah, I do think your life is like a perpetual vacation, and I'm actually jealous of it, if I'm being honest. I mean, I know you have bills and problems like everyone else, but your life is pretty great. And mine sucks. It sucked even before I got laid off and dumped and evicted. I mean, it's pretty telling that out of everything I lost, what I miss most is the apartment, you know?"

Maya managed a half grin. "Do you realize you've only mentioned Grant once or twice the whole time you've been here? I wondered if that was because you weren't ready to talk about him or if it meant something deeper."

"You know, if you had asked me a month ago, I would have told you I was in love with him and I wanted us to have a future together. But now, having had some time to step back and really think about that relationship and see it for what it was...I think I loved the *idea* of Grant more than I loved the person. I liked that he had traveled all over the world, and that he had this job that seemed important, and he seemed to know something about everything."

"He was an obnoxious arse who thought he knew way more than he did."

"I can see that now. And I think I saw it before, but we'd only been going out a few months when he got the

London offer, and it gave our relationship this urgency. Like, we had to make a commitment before it was too late."

"He was going to London, not off to war. You guys weren't even talking about serious commitments prior to that."

"I know. But then he needed someone to stay in his apartment while he was gone to take care of his plants, and my lease was ending at my place, and it seemed like it was the right thing to do at the time. Like maybe it was meant to be. Now, I think if he hadn't left, we probably wouldn't have stayed together. We had nothing in common. Two people couldn't be more opposite. And for months now, we barely talked at all. It was like the phone calls and video chats were more of an obligation than something either of us looked forward to."

"So, why did you stay in it so long?"

Katie stood and walked over to the window to look down at the parking lot. "I've thought a lot about that too. I think it just felt nice to be in a relationship, you know? Like, even if he wasn't here and we weren't able to do things together, I had a boyfriend. Sort of. And now, I don't have anyone."

"You got me, kid! And you don't have to be in a relationship to be happy. You know that, right? You need to figure out what makes you happy—you, just you. All by yourself. And then, if you find someone you want to spend your time with, and somehow, the two of you are happier together, that's icing on the cake. But don't ever stay in it if it doesn't make your life better. I mean, obviously, everyone's going to go through challenges, but being in a relationship should never make you make feel lonelier than being alone."

"I don't know what kind of pain meds they gave you, but you sound like some wise old sage."

"I'm this wise all the time. You just haven't been listening."

Katie smiled and sat on the edge of Maya's hospital bed. "I really am sorry I said those things. I love your life, and I love you. And when I grow up, I wanna be more like you and less like me."

THREE

The next day, Katie offered to cover the shop so Maya could stay home and off her foot, but Maya insisted she would be miserable cooped up in the house.

They settled her into a chair with her foot propped up, and by the time Katie left to get them both lunch, it seemed that half the town had come in to check on Maya and wish her well.

Katie had no idea how news had traveled so fast, but it warmed her heart to see how many people cared about her sister's wellbeing and how many of Maya's friends offered to help her out.

"I just got off the phone with the travel agent," Maya said when Katie came in with their lunch. "It's too close to the ship's departure date to get my money back. If I cancel, I'm out the full amount. The only thing they can refund is the shore excursions."

"That sucks. Maybe I should go and pretend to be you," Katie joked with a grin as she pulled the chicken salad wrap from the paper bag and walked it over to Maya.

"Funny you should mention that," Maya said,

returning the grin as she thanked Katie and took the sandwich. "When she said I couldn't get my money back, I asked if I could transfer the cruise and have someone else go in my place. And she said yes. I'd just have to pay one-hundred dollars for the name change."

"Yeah, but then you have to find someone who can take the time off to go on a cruise with only a two-week notice. Someone who won't mind sharing a room with your friend Ben. And someone who would be willing to pretend to be his girlfriend. Good luck finding someone dumb enough to agree to all that! I still can't believe you agreed to it!"

Maya's grin widened. "Ideally, it would be someone who didn't have a job commitment so they could easily go with short notice. Someone I'd trust to do right by Ben. Someone who really needs a vacation and some tropical vibes right about now."

"Why are you looking at me like that?" Katie said around the bite she'd just taken, her sandwich still held in mid-air.

"Because this is the perfect opportunity for you!"

"For me?" Katie nearly choked on the sandwich bite and had to chug a few swallows of water before she could take a breath or speak. "Are you insane? I'm not going on a cruise with some guy I've never met."

"Technically, you have met. I'm positive he was with us that night."

"But I don't know him!"

"Yes, but I do. I've known him for years. He's literally my best friend. Like a brother to me. There is no one else on the planet I would trust more with my baby sister than Ben."

"Well, that's great. I'm glad to know you have such high standards for sending me out to sea. But you're out of your mind if you think I'm going on a cruise with a total stranger, and you're extra insane if you think I'd be down for playing the girlfriend character in whatever scheme y'all have concocted. No. Absolutely not. Besides, don't you think Ben would have some opinion about this? He might want to choose his own roommate and pretend love interest. So, turn off the heat on whatever plan you've got cooking in your head. This ain't happening."

"Why not?" Maya leaned forward in her chair, her eyes bright with enthusiasm. "It's a weeklong vacation with all expenses paid, Kate. All you can eat. Whatever shore excursions you want to do. Tropical islands. Gorgeous views. I can't think of anyone who deserves a vacation more than you do right now. Think of all the reading you could do while relaxing on the deck. You might even get some writing done. Or not, if you don't want to think about that right now. This would be the perfect getaway for you to be able to chill out and find yourself."

"Find myself? By pretending to be someone else? Are you listening to the words coming out of your mouth right now? I can't believe you'd even suggest this. You're the one who does crazy stuff, not me. No way. Nope. Like I said, not happening."

"C'mon. At least think about it. You'd have the time of your life. I'm certain of it. You've always wanted to travel, and you've been telling me for years you want to go on a cruise. Well, here it is. Here's your opportunity, and it's already paid for. I won't get my money back either way. I'd rather you go and enjoy yourself."

"Yes, I want to travel, and yes, I'd love to go on a cruise. With *you*. With *my sister*. Not with some random guy I've never met." She held up her hand as Maya started to protest. "Okay, even if you're right and we met one time for a brief encounter that I have no memory of, it doesn't matter. I don't know the guy."

"What if we do a video chat with him, and I can reintroduce the two of you? I'm sure you'll hit it off with him the same way I did. He's a great guy, Kate. I'm telling you, this is the big brother we always wanted and never had."

"I never wanted a brother, and even if I had, I certainly wouldn't want to pretend to be his girlfriend. Ew! Look, I'm sure he's a great guy. A great guy who's using his best friend to lie to his parents, but hey...like you said. I'm a bit of a stickler for honesty and you, well, you're more flexible with the concept. But just because he's a great guy doesn't mean I want to share a room with him. End of discussion."

A customer entered the store before Maya could respond, and much to Katie's surprise, Maya let it go and didn't bring it up again the rest of the day.

It was actually Katie who mentioned it later that night as she helped Maya navigate her usual nighttime routine with the injured foot.

"Thanks, Kate," Maya said once they'd gotten her out of her clothes and into her pajamas. "I really appreciate your help."

"You don't have to thank me." Katie reached to pull back the covers on Maya's bed. "You certainly couldn't manage on your own, which is another reason it would be ludicrous for me to go on that cruise. You need me here."

"No, because if you wanted to do it, I'd ask a friend to come and stay with me. And like you said, I'll be getting around better by then anyway, so it'd be fine." Maya put her arm around her sister's shoulder and together, they managed to get her onto the bed. "It's all good, though. I understand you not wanting to go. I'm sorry if it seemed I was pressuring you earlier."

"It's not that I don't want to go on a cruise. I'd love for us to do that someday. But I don't want to go with a stranger and pretend to be his girlfriend."

"I get that," Maya said as she adjusted the pillows behind her to sit against the headboard. "I just wanted it to work out for both of you. For Ben, I know he needs a distraction to help deal with his family drama. And for you, I know you need an escape right now."

"Which is why I'm here. This is my escape."

"Yeah, but it's not the same. When you're on a ship, there is nothing around you but endless blue water and blue sky. It's so peaceful. It's like you leave the world behind when you go out there. You're able to truly disconnect. No cell phones. No emails. No *Mother*," Maya said with an exaggerated emphasis and a conspiratorial grin.

"Ugh." Katie rolled her eyes. "She called three times today. Once to tell me about a job opportunity in publishing she saw online, once to tell me some friend of hers has a daughter who does resumés, and then the third time to ask if I'd heard from Grant because she saw a guy on television who reminded her of him. I think she's more upset about our break-up than I am."

"Why do you answer her calls? Let her go to voice mail."

"Won't she just keep calling?"

"Yeah, but then eventually you call her back and she's forgotten half the stuff she wanted to tell you. It's much easier that way."

Maya winced as she lifted her foot for Katie to put a pillow underneath it.

"I still feel guilty that you wouldn't let me call them when you went into surgery," Katie said with a frown. "Are you really not going to tell her about your injury?"

"Are you kidding me?" Maya scoffed. "She'd be in the car on her way down here, and then we'd both have to deal with her."

"Good point. I'm already worried she's gonna show up and put me in her car to drive me back to New York, so yeah, probably best you don't give her any additional reason to come visit."

"I tell Mom what she needs to know, and she doesn't need to know a whole lot about my life. If it doesn't affect her, and it would make her worry obsessively—which would then make her bug me obsessively—she doesn't need to know."

"I guess I do that too, to some extent. I just haven't mastered it as well as you.'

"Stick around a while." Grinning, Maya winked. "I'll teach you all sorts of things."

There was a time when Katie would have laughed at the idea of Maya being able to teach her anything. For most of their lives, they'd been cast in roles of one having it together and the other not, and Katie had been sure of her role. But now, she'd begun to question it all.

Maya's unstructured approach to life seemed to have brought her a sense of joy and contentment Katie had never experienced. Perhaps she could stand to learn a few lessons from her free-spirited sister after all.

Her thoughts turned to the cruise, and part of her wished she had Maya's courage so she could just throw all caution to the wind and go.

"I'm sorry you're gonna miss your trip," she said. "I know you were looking forward to it. Did you tell Ben you can't go?"

"No. Not yet. I don't want to bum him out."

"You think he's gonna be pretty disappointed, huh?"

Maya shrugged as she twisted her long, curly hair into a loose bun. "Yeah. I mean, he'll be fine. He's a grown man. It's not like he can't go away with his family for a week without emotional support. But Ben's kind of like me in that being around his mom gets him all worked up and stressed out. I volunteered to go so he'd have an outlet. Someone there who understands. Someone he can vent to who would get it."

"He's lucky to have a friend like you."

"Oh, please," Maya chuckled as she waved off that assertion. "It's not like it would be a hardship to go on vacation for a week. I would have had a great time! You know me— I'm always up for an adventure."

"Yes, you are. That's something I admire about you."

"You're adventurous, too."

"Ha! Hardly."

"You moved to New York right out of college all by yourself."

"Yeah, but I had a job offer lined up, and that girl I knew from school had offered me a room, so I knew I had a place to stay. It's not like I packed up a car and took off without a plan."

"It doesn't make it any less adventurous just because you did it the smart way. There are plenty of people who never leave their hometown or the state they were born in. You had a dream, you made a plan, and you went after it. That's adventurous."

"But I still failed."

Maya's eyes widened. "What? You didn't *fail*, Kate."

"Whatever," Katie huffed.

"No, not whatever. You didn't fail. This wasn't a test like when you were in school. You don't get a bad grade when things don't pan out the way you'd hoped."

Katie responded with silence and a subtle shake of her head.

"Hey, listen to me," Maya said, leaning forward to lay her hand on Katie's arm. "You did *not* fail. It's not your fault you got laid off because of budget cuts. It's not your fault Grant was a jerk. Sometimes, things happen that we have no control over, okay? I know that's hard for you, Miss Always-Has-A-Plan, but there's no pass or fail. There's just life. When it doesn't go the way you wanted it to, you learn what you can from it and move on."

"But I worked so hard, Maya." Katie plopped down on the bed next to her sister. "I put everything I had into getting to New York. Into getting that job. And now, I have nothing to show for it. All that time, and it's just...gone."

"Oh, sweetie. The time may be gone, and the job may be gone, but the experience isn't. You still lived it. That's what life is. The experience. Some days are better than others, but all of it means something. Every single day, no matter where we are and what we're doing, we feel, we grow, we learn. We live. And there's a lot of trial and error in that. You tried something, and it didn't work out. So now, you try something else. And it may not work out either. And if it doesn't, you try something else. That's living."

"Great. Living is a string of failures. Can't wait."

Maya grinned. "No. Living is a string of experiences. Love. Laughter. Heartache. Triumph. Disappointment. Joy. All of it. It's all about the experiences."

Katie had bent her head, allowing her hair to fall forward in hopes it would hide her silent tears, but Maya pulled the strands back and tucked them behind Katie's ear as she leaned in closer.

"I know thinking of New York right now is painful, and

I know even the good memories seem tainted by the way it all ended. But I want you to try and focus on those good ones. The things you loved about it. The things you want to carry forward."

"Carry forward?" Katie asked, tilting her head to look at Maya.

"Yeah. On our life journey, there are things we leave behind, and things we carry forward. New York, for now, you leave behind. But you'll always have those memories and the things you carry forward from your time there."

"You mean, like, stuff I bought there?"

Maya shrugged. "It can be something tangible, sure, but it doesn't have to be. Maybe it's a new cuisine you tried and loved, or a new style of music you found there. It could be the influence the city had on your fashion. Maybe it's the croissant at a cafe you'll always remember. Or the glow of the sunset coming through the window of your apartment. You see, we pick up things from every adventure, every relationship, every job, every city. Even books, movies, songs, paintings. It all shapes us and shapes our journey. So, New York isn't a failure. It's just part of your journey. It's part of who you are now. It shaped you. And you get to decide where your journey takes you next and what you want to carry forward with you."

For the first time since she'd arrived at Maya's, sleep eluded Katie. Her mind churned, thoughts racing in all directions as she replayed her life journey and contemplated where she wanted to go next.

It was hard not to compare her journey with Maya's. While she didn't envy the hardships Maya had gone through, and she wouldn't have wanted to experience Maya's struggles, she wished she had Maya's easygoing nature, her courage, and her ability to take life as it comes and find the good in it all.

Katie's life had always been planned three steps ahead of where she was. No decision was made without thorough research, deep contemplation, and a careful analysis of all possible outcomes. No idea was considered worthwhile unless it moved her toward a desired goal or achievement.

And then, if that goal or achievement wasn't acquired, she beat herself up and felt like she'd let herself—and others —down. Like she'd failed.

But if it went well, she was already onto the next goal. The next achievement. The next chase.

What would it be like to just...live? If her measure of success in life wasn't based on a particular achievement or goal, how would she know if she was doing well? If she was doing it...*right*?

Her whole life had been spent trying to do the *right* thing.

Was Maya correct in her assumption that there wasn't a right or wrong—there was just life?

Maya certainly seemed more at peace living her way than Katie had ever been living hers.

But was Katie even capable of being more like Maya?

She'd always been told by her parents that they were wired differently. They said Maya was wired to be rebellious and free-spirited, while Katie was wired to obedient and driven. But did that mean Maya was wired to be content and happy while Katie was destined to feel like nothing was ever quite enough?

What would it be like to do something purely for the

fun of doing it, without considering every possible long-term consequence or outcome?

What would Katie's life be like if she could do something just because she wanted to, and not because she was supposed to?

To some extent, she'd done that in moving back to Florida to stay with Maya. Everyone—especially her mother—had expected her to stay in New York and find another job. They'd wanted her to pursue the same path she'd been trudging along for years. But instead, she'd cast it all aside to join Maya at the surf shop.

And since making that choice, she'd felt lighter and more at peace than she had in years.

The move was temporary, of course, but she had to admit that now having veered off that defined path, she didn't feel any desire to return to it. If anything, she felt more intrigued by how far away from it she could go.

Maya had asked what she would carry with her, but at the moment, Katie was more interested in determining what else she wanted to leave behind. Maybe it was time to shed more than just New York, publishing, and Grant.

She felt like she had gotten a second chance to choose her path. The rest of her life lay before her, and while she wasn't sure yet what direction it would take, she made a promise that from now on, she'd spend more time focused on the journey instead of having tunnel vision for the destination.

Four

"I wanna go on the cruise," Katie told Maya the next morning in such an abrupt about-face that Maya nearly choked on the pancakes Katie had made them.

"What?" Maya managed to get out once she'd swallowed. "What brought that on?"

"I was just thinking about my life last night after we talked. What I've been doing so far hasn't worked out so well for me. So going forward, I want to be more adventurous. More spontaneous. I wanna be more like you."

"Like me? No, no, no." Maya shook her head with an exaggerated fervor. "You don't want to be more like me. I don't know what you took from what I said last night, but that wasn't my intent. And I didn't say any of it to get you to go on the cruise."

"I know that."

"Look, I just wanted you to lighten up on yourself and not take life so seriously. I wanted you to see that it's not a failure if things don't go the way you planned. 'Cause, unfortunately, that's gonna happen. A lot. I do want you to enjoy your life more, and while I agree it would be great if you could work in some spontaneity and adventure along the way, you don't need to be like me. You're perfectly wonderful exactly the way you are."

"But I'm not happy the way I am. I don't know that I've ever really been happy, Maya. I feel like I've always been working toward being happy and thinking it would happen once I got to wherever I was headed. But every time I reached one goal, I always had another one lined up, and I never figured out the point where I was allowed to be happy."

Maya slid her hand across the table toward her sister.

"Oh, Kate. You can be happy anywhere, anytime."

"Maybe *you* can, but not me. I'm not sure I even know how to be. But I want to be. In less than three years, I'll be thirty. If I haven't figured it out by now, then obviously I need to change what I'm doing. And from where I'm sitting, you seem pretty happy. So...yeah. I wanna be more like you."

"No." Maya shook her head again. "I am a complete screw-up. I always have been. You know that."

"You're not, though. What you are is a light in the darkness. You have this joy—this light—that radiates from you. Everyone sees it. It's why they all smile when you're around. Even strangers. You're contagious. And while I was chasing one goal after another, you were learning how to enjoy life in the moment and find your peace. I got it all wrong, and you...you've done it right. Teach me how to live that way."

"Good Lord, Kate, I have not done it right. I've screwed up every way a person can, okay? But each day when I get up, I try to do better than I did the day before. Every single day, I look for things to be grateful for, things to enjoy, things to appreciate. I make a point of smiling, even when I may not feel like it, and on the days when it's particularly hard, I focus on making others smile because that makes it easier for me to do it." She smiled at Katie as though to demonstrate her point, and then she took her napkin from her lap and folded it on the table. "But there's nothing wrong with you or the way you've done things, okay? Goals are good. I've got goals. I've got plans. And maybe I'll get around to them all eventually. But you...you make stuff happen for real. You're a goal-oriented person. Always have been. You're one of the smartest people I've ever known. You're a hard worker. You're resourceful. You're more organized than I'll ever be. That jerk you worked for and that scumbag you dated didn't see what a gem they had, but that doesn't diminish your value. I don't want you down on yourself or wanting to change who you are because of them."

"It's not because of them. Really, it's not. I think I've known for a while that I needed a change. Getting laid off and having Grant end things was a wake-up call that now's the time. And being here with you just makes it easier to see that there's another way to live. I'm not saying I'm out to change everything about me or become a totally different person. But I want to learn how to be happy. How to appreciate the present moment and be content being in it without always looking toward some future moment that may not come to pass."

Maya nodded slowly and then cocked her head to the side. "Okay, I hear you, and I'm happy to help however I can. Whatever I can offer, whatever you can learn from me, it's yours. But I'm not sure I understand what any of this has to do with the cruise. You were so adamantly opposed before. Why do you want to go now?"

"Because it's something that the old Katie would never in a million years do, and I want the new Katie to be the kind of person who would at least consider it. Like I said, I want to be more spontaneous. Adventurous. More willing to step outside my comfort zone and have new experiences I didn't plan for. This is the beginning of a new chapter for me, and I can't think of a better way to start it than to sail away from my past and spend a week focused solely on having fun."

"Well, all right!" Maya said, her grin spreading. "That's the spirit!"

"But are you sure Ben will be okay with me being your substitute? I know you said he and I met, but he may not remember either. And even if he does, I'm still a stranger, so he may feel the same way I did and not want me to go."

"I'm thinking Ben would rather spend time with a stranger than be stuck alone on a ship with his family. It's six hours ahead in Barcelona, so he's still at the gallery, but he may be able to talk. Let's call him."

"No, we shouldn't call him if he's working."

"He's not like Grant, okay? If he's busy, he'll either let it go to voice mail or he'll answer and say he can't talk."

"Okay, well, you call him. I don't want to put him on the spot by listening in. I need to get in the shower anyway. And hey, I mean it, if he's not comfortable with this, I won't go. It's fine.

"Hey! Ben wants to talk to you," Maya called out as Katie stepped from the shower a few minutes later.

"What?" Katie clutched the towel around her, feeling exposed even though she was alone in the bathroom. "Why?"

"Maybe because the two of you are planning to go on a cruise together, and I guess he wants to say *hi*?"

Tucking the towel into itself so that it wouldn't fall, Katie opened the door and frowned at Maya. "I don't know what to say," she whispered.

"Say *hi* back."

Katie took the phone from Maya with a frown. "Uh, hi."

"Hi! It's Ben, though I guess you already knew that. Is Maya still close by? Can she hear you?"

"Yeah."

"Can you go somewhere she can't hear you?"

Katie frowned again and then walked to her bedroom and shut the door. "Okay. She can't hear me."

"All right. Then I need you to tell me the truth. Do you really want to go on this cruise?"

Katie stared at the ceiling as she considered her answer. "Um, yeah, I guess. I think so. Why?"

"Is Maya making you do this? Is she bribing you or blackmailing you or something?"

"Wow. You really do know my sister well," Katie said with a chuckle.

"I'm not saying anything negative about Maya. I just want to make sure she isn't talking you into doing something you don't want to do. I know she feels bad that she isn't able to come, and I know how persuasive she can be when she wants something. Is this your decision or hers?"

"Oh. It's mine. She does feel bad, and believe me, I know all about Maya's skills with persuasion, but I think I built up an immunity to them in high school. Trust me when I say no one does peer pressure as well as my sister, but I learned how to resist her. So, yeah. I'd like to go on the cruise. I mean, if that's okay with you. And if it's not, I totally understand. We don't know each other, so if it seems too awkward..."

"No, it's fine. It may be a bit awkward, but hey, I'm up for it if you are. She did tell you we'd be sharing a room, right? Twin beds, though, and I swear I'll be the perfect gentleman. I'll leave the room whenever you need to change or shower, or anything like that."

The feeling of being exposed returned, and she hugged the towel more tightly around her, not willing to drop it to get dressed even though there was no way Ben could see her. She couldn't believe she was doing this. She was actually making arrangements to share a tiny cabin on a ship—and a tiny bathroom—with a stranger.

But if she was going to bring adventure into her life, she had to start somewhere. At least Ben was someone Maya knew and trusted.

"Yeah, she did tell me it was one room. As far as privacy goes, I'll do the same. I can step out whenever you need me to."

"All right, then." They both fell silent for a moment's pause, and then Ben continued. "Katie, if you don't mind my asking, why do you want to do this?"

She sat on the bed and looked around the tiny room that had been her safe haven since she fled New York. *How much of her life did she want to share with this stranger?*

It was probably best to keep it minimal. She didn't want him to worry he'd be confined for a week with a depressed, blubbering mess. And she didn't think she'd be that. She'd gotten much better since she'd been in Florida.

"I see it as an adventure," she said with complete honesty. "I'm eager to know what it's like to cruise, and I've never visited any of the islands, so that's exciting."

"You've never been on a cruise?"

"No. I've never really been anywhere."

"Maya said you lived in New York."

"Yeah, and I spent a weekend in London once, but it wasn't...it was...never mind. It doesn't matter."

Good grief, she thought. *Why bring that up? Could I be any more awkward?*

"New York and London are both wonderful cities," Ben said. "Nothing in the Caribbean is quite that big, I'm afraid, but the islands have their own charm, and of course, beautiful scenery."

"I'm looking forward to seeing them."

"Good. Now, Maya went for the most adrenaline-filled excursion option in each port, but she said you might like something more...cultural. So, if you want to take a look at the ship's website, you can see all the options and decide if there are any you'd like to do."

"Would we be doing those together?" she asked, knowing he and Maya had planned to do so, but unsure of how it would work between the two of them.

"We can, if you'd like. I didn't know if you'd rather do them on your own."

"Oh. But won't your family think it's odd if we aren't together? Maya told me they'll expect...well, that the two of you planned to act like you were dating."

"Yeah...about that..." Ben cleared his throat before continuing. "Maya had suggested that she say she was my girlfriend, but I wouldn't expect you to do that. That's asking a bit much."

Katie exhaled in relief. That was the part of the deal she was most uncomfortable with.

"I'm fine with saying we're friends," Ben offered. "Maybe we could not mention that we've only met once though? It's just that...I don't know. I worry my mother will make it difficult no matter what we say, and I hate that."

"Would it really be so bad to tell the truth? Why lie about having a girlfriend? Why lie to them at all?"

"Valid questions, for sure, and I can see how it would seem like a bad idea. It wasn't something I set out to do. You see, my mother can be rather...*intrusive*...in my life, so I choose to be guarded with the information I share."

"I get that. I'm sure Maya has told you about our mom."

"A bit, yes." Ben chuckled. "My mother is very set in her thinking of what my life should look like. I've already disappointed her by being an artist rather than a lawyer, and then I had the audacity to reach the ripe of old age of thirty-one without being married yet. My career choice she took as insult to my father, but my relationship status—she takes that one as a personal slight, as though the only reason I'm single is to defy her wishes on the matter."

Katie had been dealing with her mother's grief over the relationship with Grant ending for days, and though Rosalyn hadn't come right out and said the words, she'd insinuated that Katie's time was running out due to thirty looming on the not-so-distant horizon.

"I can relate, even though I'm only twenty-seven, which is obviously *much* younger than thirty-one," she teased. "My situation isn't nearly as dire as the point you're at."

Ben's laugh was quick and hearty, and it made Katie smile.

"Yes, well, being as over the hill as I am and still single, I dared to think I could embark upon this family cruise unaccompanied," he said. "But then my mother offered to invite a guest along for me."

"Maya mentioned that. Your ex-girlfriend, I believe?"

"Yes. Allison. A lovely woman who is my ex for a reason, but my mother has never given up hope that we'll end up together. And when I say *never given up hope*, I mean she tries to force the situation every chance she gets. So, in a moment of panic, I told Mother she couldn't invite Allison because I was already bringing someone. And in my scramble afterward to determine who this non-existent person might be, your sister came to my rescue and said that she would be happy to accompany me, but only if I let her play the part of my doting lover."

"An enthusiastic, doting lover, I'm sure."

"Oh, yes. I have no doubt. As you obviously know, Maya does nothing without enthusiasm. And since we've already discussed your sister's master levels at persuasion—"

"She talked you into it."

"Yeah, but it wasn't like it was a hard sell. I knew I'd have a great time with Maya, and I didn't have any other prospects for a cruise companion. Even if I had been seeing someone, it's one thing to go on a cruise with a girl you're interested in when it's just the two of you. Inviting her on a family vacation sends a whole different message about where the relationship might be headed."

"I can see where that would take *meeting the parents* to the next level."

"To an extreme level for a first-time meeting, but with Maya willing to step in, there was no pressure. My mother would have a bone to chew on, and Maya would have a blast screwing with her. And then we'd get off the ship, and if Mother ever asked, I'd say that Maya and I decided to be friends, and no one would ever be the wiser."

Katie wasn't surprised her sister would be willing to put on a performance, but was this a role Katie could play?

Could she pretend they were anything other than strangers? Could she lie to people she'd never even met?

It wasn't like she'd ever see his family again after this trip. What did it matter if they thought she and Ben were dating for the week? She didn't have to marry him or anything. She just had to pretend she knew him better than she did.

"Okay, I guess I'll do it," she said with a sigh.

"Whoa, now." Ben laughed softly. "Temper that excitement a little. Don't sound too eager."

"I just don't know if I can pull it off. I'm not the actress Maya is."

"And that's okay. I'm not asking you to be. I told my mother I was bringing someone, but I didn't say it was a girlfriend, and I didn't offer any details. I was willing to go along with Maya's idea because she wanted to do it, and it seemed like fun, quite honestly. But since she's not coming, I'll tell them you and I are just friends."

Katie felt an odd pang of rejection, possibly triggered by years of being known as the less fun sister, and perhaps amplified by Grant's betrayal being so recent. Not being wanted hurt, even it was only as an imaginary love interest.

"Fine. It's not like it was something I wanted to do. I was just trying to help."

"No, I get that. I know. And I appreciate that you'd be willing to do it. Truly. But I wouldn't ask that of you."

"Kate?" Maya called out from the living room. "You ready?"

Katie glanced at the clock on the nightstand, cursing beneath her breath as she dropped the towel and pulled a bra and panties from the dresser drawer.

"I gotta go. We have to open the surf shop, and I don't have any clothes on." Warmth flooded her cheeks as she realized what she'd revealed. "I mean, I'm...I've been wearing a towel while we were talking. Only because I just got out of the shower. And I have no idea why I'm telling you any of this, so I'm just gonna go crawl under a rock and die of embarrassment now."

She slapped her palm against her forehead as Ben's laughter rang out.

"Don't worry about it," he said. "I'll let you get on with your day, but if you think of anything else we need to discuss, feel free to give me a call or a text. Maya has my number."

"Right. Okay. Gotta go. Bye."

"Kate?" Maya called again, and Katie flung the bedroom door open even though she was only wearing a bra and panties.

"I'm coming."

"You're not even dressed?" Maya shuffled down the hall with her injured leg kneeling on the knee scooter. "What have you been doing?"

"Talking to Ben! What do you think?" Katie yanked a T-shirt over her head and pulled on a pair of denim shorts, thankful she no longer had to wear business attire every day. "You're ready to go? Like, teeth brushed, shoes on, everything? Why didn't you wait for me to help you?"

"Because I need to do things for myself. I still haven't gotten used to this stupid cart though, and I keep forgetting my foot is sticking out behind me. I bumped into the table in my room and knocked the lamp off."

"Oh, no! Did it break?"

"Yes, but on the bright side, I never really liked that lamp anyway. I got a great deal on it at a thrift store, and I always meant to repaint it but never had gotten around to it. Now, I don't have to! Problem solved. So...tell me...what did you think of Ben?"

"He seemed nice enough, not that you can really judge someone's character based on one short phone conversation," Katie said as she yanked a comb through her hair and then pulled it up into a ponytail, which she wrapped with an elastic band.

"Are you going?"

"Yeah." She took a deep breath as she stared at her reflection in the mirror. "It's completely nuts, but I'm going on a cruise for a week with a stranger."

Maya grinned as their eyes met in the mirror. "Welcome to the next chapter of your life!"

FIVE

Ben called Maya and asked to speak to Katie about an hour after they'd gotten the surf shop open.

"Hey, I've been thinking more about the shore excursions," he said. "If you don't see an activity you like in St. Maarten, we could always book a taxi and see a bit of the island. I spent some time there one summer, and I have a few favorite spots I could show you. I mean, if you want. And not to say we have to spend time together off the ship. You can do your own thing, of course. I was just saying, you know, it's an option."

"An island tour sounds nice. I'll look at the excursions later and let you know what I'm interested in, and we can decide from there. If there's something we both want to do, I'm happy to go together."

"Great. Why don't you text me the ones you like, and I'll take a look and get back to you? And I'm sure Maya probably told you, but the whole reason for this torture trip is my five-year-old nephew's birthday. Brady remembers visiting a turtle conservation center on St Thomas when they cruised two years ago, and he asked to go back for his birthday. So, my sister chose this ship because it will stop at St. Thomas on Wednesday, which is Brady's birthday, and she spoke with the turtle center and arranged for the family to celebrate there. Obviously, you don't have to go, but I wanted to let you know my family might expect to see you there. Even if we're only friends."

"Right. No, that makes sense. I'll plan to be there."

"Thanks." He paused for a moment. "I appreciate what you're doing. That you're willing to come along and be up for whatever the adventure brings. I think that's really cool of you, and I promise I'll do my best to show you a good time so you don't regret coming."

"Thanks, but I'm sure it'll be great."

"Well, if it isn't, we both know your sister will have my head. So, there's that."

She laughed and assured him that wasn't the case, and then they said goodbye.

With the decision made, Katie threw herself into planning for the cruise. It would be her first vacation as an adult since she didn't count the disastrous weekend in London where all she did was stay indoors nursing an ailing Grant.

With only two weeks to prepare, she felt a sense of urgency that drove her to study the cruise website like she was cramming for an exam. She memorized the ship's layout and made note of the restaurants and stores she wanted to visit, and then she turned her attention to the island destinations they'd be visiting: Charlotte Amalie, St. Thomas; Philipsburg, St. Maarten; and Coconut Palms Cay, Bahamas, which was the cruise line's private island resort.

Over the next few days, she and Ben texted back and forth regarding the available excursions and activities along with other details regarding the trip. They decided to book snorkeling together at Coconut Palms Cay, and then Ben would be her tour guide on St. Maarten. Brady's birthday celebration would take up the afternoon they were on St. Thomas, but Katie booked a solo seat on a historic bus tour that morning so she could see more of the island.

Without the pressure of the girlfriend ruse, she found it much easier to be excited about the trip. The concept of sharing a room with Ben still felt awkward, but their text conversations had at least helped to break the ice between them so he no longer seemed like a complete stranger. Katie just wished they could have more time to get to know each other in person before they got on the ship. He was scheduled to fly into Miami the night before their departure, and then she would fly to Miami to meet him the morning of the cruise, giving them very little time to get used to one another before they were thrown together in a cabin.

He'd offered to change his flight to come into Orlando instead, which would allow them to meet the night before and either fly or drive to Miami together. But it made no sense to uproot all his plans for what essentially would only be a few hours spent together, so Katie kept things the way they were.

"I'm sorry I can't drive you to the airport myself," Maya said the morning of the cruise. "I swear not being able to drive is almost as bad as not being to surf or run. I don't know how you did without a car in New York."

"I didn't need one, so I didn't miss it." Katie finished applying one last coat of mascara and then tossed the tube into her cosmetics bag. "I could walk almost everywhere I needed to get to, and there were always taxis, buses, and the subway for anywhere too far to go on foot."

"You sure you don't want me to ride with you and Mel?"

"No, I'm good. There's no reason for you to close the shop just to go to the airport. I've flown by myself plenty of times."

She tossed the cosmetics case into her carry-on bag and zipped it shut.

"Did you remember to put a change of clothes in there for dinner?" Maya asked, pointing toward the bag.

"Yes, *Mom*. I did exactly what you told me. I packed a change of clothes, my toothbrush and toothpaste, and my swimsuit and a cover-up in the carry-on in case my luggage is delivered late. Although I can't see myself rushing to put on a bathing suit as soon as we get on the boat."

"You never know. You guys might decide to sit by the pool or in the hot tub. It's best to be prepared."

"Oh my goodness, what's happening here?" Katie said, laying her hand on her chest in mock shock. "Did we get zapped by some freaky spell and switch places? I'm running off on a cruise with a stranger, and you're spouting packing advice and telling me to be prepared?"

"Very funny," Maya said with a grin. "I'll have you know I'm an excellent and efficient packer. I'd never be dragging a bag that big." She pointed to Katie's large suitcase by the door. "I went to Europe for two months with nothing but a backpack."

"Yeah, well, backpacking when you're staying in hostels is one thing. I need enough clothes for every occasion—snorkeling, island tours, pool days, a child's birthday party, and dinner with Ben's parents, whom you've both told me are pretty uptight."

The doorbell rang with Mel's arrival, and Katie turned to Maya with a mixture of panic and excitement. "That's my ride. Time to go!"

Maya grinned as she hobbled forward on the knee

scooter to take Katie's hands in hers. "I want you to take every opportunity to have a great time for the next week. Make the start of this new chapter epic, and if you come home with regrets, it better not be because you missed out on something."

The sisters hugged, and then Katie loaded her bags into the back of Mel's car before coming back to the door to hug Maya one more time.

"Remember that you need to rest, okay?" Katie squeezed Maya tighter and then released her. "And no weight on that foot. Not even a little. Use the scooter, even when you think you don't need it."

"I've got it. I'm good. Delia will be here soon to drive me to the shop and help me get it open. Then she, Mel, and Beth are all gonna tag-team to make sure I've always got someone on call while you're gone. So don't worry."

"You know I will anyway."

"I know," Maya said as Katie turned to go. "Have fun for me, okay? Do something I would do. Something old Katie never would have done. That should give you plenty of options!"

The flight to Miami was short and smooth, but Katie was a bundle of nerves for the entire ride in anticipation of meeting Ben.

He was just a guy. So what if they were about to sleep in the same room together for seven nights? It didn't mean anything. It was like being assigned a random roommate in college. Except this one was of the opposite sex and handsome as hell if the pictures Maya had shown her were any indication.

She rubbed her palms over the sundress she'd borrowed from Maya as she made her way to baggage claim, wondering if she'd be able to spot him before he spotted her.

They'd texted each other a description of what they were wearing, so the moment she could see the luggage carousels up ahead, she started searching for him.

There were a surprising number of men wandering around the airport in blue and white tropical print shirts and khaki shorts, and most of them seemed to have brown hair and brown eyes. But only one matched the guy she'd seen in Maya's pictures, and at six-foot-three, he stood out among the crowd.

He was scanning for her as well, and his smile lit up his face when they made eye contact.

Wow. He was even more handsome than his pictures, and her stomach did a funny flip when she considered spending the next week by his side.

Don't be ridiculous, she told herself. *And don't be awkward.*

With one more swipe across the dress to ensure her palms didn't feel clammy, she approached him with her hand extended in greeting.

"You must be Ben. It's so nice to finally meet you. Or, um, meet you again, I suppose I should say. Maya tells me we met one time before, but I don't remember you. Not that you're forgettable. You're not. It's just that I don't... um...there were a lot of people."

Okay, too late. Already awkward.

His smile remained through the handshake, which was firm but not aggressive. "Yes, we met at the concert, and yeah, there were a lot of people. And if I remember correctly, you had some other things going on, so you might

69

have been distracted. No worries. I'm sure after the next week, you will definitely remember me. I can only hope it will be for all good reasons."

"Same." She smiled as he released her hand. "Um, meaning I hope you'll remember me for good reasons as well. That we'll both remember each other. That it'll be good."

Oh, God. Was she going to say something weird every time she opened her mouth?

"Looks like the luggage is starting to come in for your flight," Ben said, looking past her toward the carousel, which had started moving with a loud warning signal and a flash of the light above it.

Once they'd retrieved her suitcase, they made their way outside to wait for an Uber driver.

"Thanks for meeting me at the airport," Katie said. "I'm sure any driver could have gotten me to the ship's terminal without a problem, but it was cool to have a friendly face waiting when I arrived."

"Of course! I figured this would give us a chance to talk a little before we get onboard and things get underway."

"Right. Good idea. Is your family already on the ship?"

"Yes. They are in a concierge suite, so they were among the first to board this morning."

"Oh. Our room isn't on the concierge level, though. Which is fine, but are we not near them?"

"No. Definitely not." Ben indicated that their driver was approaching and then stepped forward to the curb, pulling her luggage along with his. "I booked later than they did, so the concierge level was sold out, but I probably would have chosen a different area of the ship anyway. The more difficult it is for them to come to my room, the better."

They greeted the driver, and then Ben held the car's door open for Katie as their luggage was loaded into the trunk.

"Maya said you only planned to see your family at dinner," Katie said once they were on their way to the port. "Well, other than your nephew's birthday outing."

"That's the plan. I predict that my father and my brother-in-law will stay parked in the casino any time it's open, and then take up space on a barstool any time it's not. And since I'm not a gambler and I don't drink, I won't see a lot of them. As far as my mother, she'll probably only leave her suite to go to the dining room or the spa. Unless Brady can coax her out. He holds more sway with her than anyone else."

"Why would she come on a cruise if she doesn't plan to leave her room?"

"Because Brady invited her for his birthday, and he is her only grandchild. Another way I've failed her."

"Yeah, but if she's gonna come, why stay in her room? Why not enjoy what the ship has to offer?"

"My mother doesn't like crowds. Or being around... people...in general."

"Okay, good to know. And what about your sister? What's her name again?"

"Laura. Hard to predict. She and her husband Dale have been on several cruises, so she obviously enjoys them. But she tends to stick closer to Mother when they're together, so I suspect she and Brady will spend most of their time in the suite as well."

"I saw that they have children's programs on board. Won't Brady be involved with those?"

"Hard to say. It depends on how much Laura is willing to let Brady do without her, which usually isn't a lot. But the older he gets, the more vocal the little guy's becoming about his need for independence."

Katie took a moment to digest all he'd said, and then she looked at him, her brow scrunched in confusion. "Help me understand why you'd come on a vacation with your family and plan not to see them."

Ben shrugged. "I come for the same reason my mother does. Brady. He personally invited me."

"Yeah, but what good is it to come if you're not going to spend time with him?"

"I'll spend all the time with him I can. I take whatever I can get. But I'm here because I want him to know that I show up when he asks me to. That he can count on me." He leaned over closer with a hint of a smirk playing at his lips. "As far as not spending time with the rest of my family, I think once you meet them, you'll understand why."

"I can't wait," Katie said on a loud exhale as Ben chuckled. "With the way you're making them sound, maybe my sister broke her ankle on purpose."

"Nah, I think Maya would have had a field day with them. She had all these plans of what she was going to say and what she was going to do. They wouldn't have known what to do with her, and I guiltily admit I was looking forward to it."

"She told me she'd created a character will a full back-story and everything. She would have been great at it, I'm sure. I'm sorry she couldn't come."

"Me too," Ben said, but then he flashed her an apologetic look. "But that's not to say anything negative about you being here. I always enjoy Maya's company, and I'm sure I'll enjoy yours as well."

"Oh, well, I might as well tell you now—I'm no substitute for my sister. I couldn't be if I tried. Maya has enough personality for twelve of me."

"Really? Because she's always telling me how funny you are. How smart you are. How creative you are. She thinks highly of you."

Katie shook her head with a bashful smile. "That's Maya being nice. She's always got something positive to say. I'm not nearly as funny or as creative as she is. Never have been. When we were growing up, I was always the smart one, and she was always the entertaining one. We didn't ask for those roles; we were born into them."

"Well, I, for one, think your sister is very intelligent, and I bet you are funnier than you think. You've made me laugh quite a few times already, and I've only had a handful of conversations with you. As far as creativity, you both have skills and talents, just in different mediums. You write, and she paints. One isn't any more creative than the other."

"Thanks. I appreciate you saying that, and I appreciate you letting me tag along on your horrific family vacation." She waited as Ben laughed, and then she continued, "No, but seriously. Maya told me this trip might be difficult for you, and I realize we don't know each other very well. And I get that it would be better if you had Maya with you, but I want you to know that I'll do whatever I can to be supportive or encouraging...or whatever you need. I'm here, for what it's worth."

"Thank you for that. Maya mentioned you've been going through some things lately, so I'll make the same offer. Whatever I can do, I'm here."

"Thanks." Katie turned to look out the window, curious what Maya had told him but not wanting to ask. The last thing she wanted to think about today was her problems.

"I also want to apologize ahead of time for anything my mother says or does. My sister too, just in case, though usually Laura's not so bad. She's worse when she's with Mother."

"Oh, I'm sure they'll be fine," Katie said, looking back at him.

"Trust me. You haven't met them yet, and I'm certain they'll say or do something obnoxious."

"Even if they do, that's not on you to apologize for them."

"Not even when I'm the reason you're on the receiving end of their nonsense?"

Katie shrugged. "I'd say, technically, Maya is the reason. If she hadn't broken her ankle, she'd be here instead of me."

"But Maya was only here because of me, so it's still my fault."

"How your mother and sister behave isn't your fault, Ben. They're adults. They should be responsible for their own behavior."

"No, I get that, and you're right. I'm just saying I don't know how they'll react to you. What they'll ask you. What they'll say about me bringing you."

Katie stared at him, wondering if it would really be as bad as he seemed to fear. Were they going to be rude right to her face?

"What do they normally say to people you introduce them to?"

It was Ben's turn to shrug. "I don't. I haven't brought anyone home in years. It's not worth it to me to risk someone I care about being treated unkindly."

"You care about Maya, though."

"Yeah, but Maya knew what she was getting into. Or

had a better idea, at least. She knows my family history and what I deal with. She was prepared for it."

"And you worry I won't be able to handle it?"

"I feel bad that you even have to try. Your sister was going into this expecting them to be obnoxious, and she was willing to take that and spin it back at them."

"And she could do it, for sure."

"Yes. And it might have been a disaster, but there was a part of me that wanted to see someone take my mother on. Maya didn't care what they thought of her, so she was willing to do or say anything."

Katie turned back toward the window, surprised to see they were already arriving at the cruise terminal. "That's Maya, though. She's always done and said whatever she wanted. Even when she's not pretending to be someone else. And somehow, she gets away with it."

"She's a fireball, for sure, that sister of yours. Sometimes, I wish I had her moxie—that I could care a little bit less what other people think."

"You and me both," Katie mumbled as she stared up at the massive ships, unable to believe she was about to board one. Her phone buzzed in her purse, and she pulled it out and grinned. "Speak of the devil. I forgot to call and let her know I landed. I'm gonna be in trouble now."

"Uh-oh. I'm probably in trouble too for not reminding you to do it."

"Hey, sorry, I forgot to call you," Katie said to Maya. "I'm here. I'm with Ben, and we're pulling up to get out at the cruise terminal now."

"I figured y'all got to talking and forgot me already, but I wanted to catch you before you get onboard. Put me on speaker."

Katie did as Maya asked and then told her to go ahead.

"Ben? You better take care of my baby sister, or I will hunt you down," Maya said. "I have a very particular set of skills, and I'm not afraid to use them."

Katie grinned at the Uber driver's nervous glance in the rearview mirror, and she wondered if he realized it was a movie quote. Not exactly an empty threat where Maya was concerned, but not as dangerous as it sounded.

"And Kate? You take care of my buddy, and you don't let that family of his bring him down, okay? If they start in on him, you have my permission to channel me and go at them full blast. And if they bring you down, I'm going after them with that set of skills I mentioned."

"Can you not just say *Bon voyage* or *have a great time* like a normal person?" Katie asked with an eyeroll.

"Sure! *Bon voyage!* Now, you two go get on that ship and have the most wonderful time you can without me, because obviously you both know you'd have a better time with me."

"But, of course," Ben said with a huge smile. "We're gonna miss ya, but I promise to take good care of your sister. Thanks for loaning her to me."

"You better bring her back in one piece, and she better have nothing but great stories to tell. Take lots of pictures. I love you both!"

Six

Katie's excitement level built as they went through the check-in process at the cruise terminal, and by the time they began their walk through the long glass tunnel to board the ship, she was nearly giddy with delight.

"I can't believe I'm going on a vacation. I'm going on a ship. A cruise! I'm going to the Caribbean."

Ben chuckled at her enthusiasm. "Yes, you are. Did you just realize this now?"

"No, but I haven't really let myself get too hyped up about it. I'm always wary of getting my hopes up for something and then being disappointed and having to rein it all back in. And with this, there was so much chaos around it. I'd just moved to Maya's when she got injured, and between helping her get around, pitching in to run the store, and then deciding to take this trip, it's been nuts. And even though I was excited to go, I was also scrambling to figure it all out and get things booked with such short notice, so it was stressful." She turned to face him, walking almost sideways to do so. "But now, it's here, and I'm here, and I'm like ultra-psyched. I can't believe I'm actually doing this."

"You're doing it."

"I'm doing it." Her grin widened as she straightened and faced forward again. "We're checked in. We're boarding. Look, this ID card has my name on it." She held up the card for him to see. "This is happening!"

"Yeah, it is," Ben said, his grin never wavering. "I used to do that—keep myself in check so I didn't get my hopes up. But a wise friend told me that when we live that way, we're focusing more on the disappointment than the joy. She says you should assume it's going to be good, and then, if something doesn't work out, you just deal with the disappointment. But at least you got to be happy part of the time."

"Geez, do I happen to know this *wise friend* of yours? Because that sounds exactly like something Maya would say."

Ben laughed. "You guessed it. That's definitely Maya's influence. Before we became friends, I was always the type who would figure out the worst-case scenario and plan for that so I could feel like I was prepared no matter what happened."

"Which is exactly how I am," Katie said with a sigh.

"But that's not how Maya lives."

"No. Certainly not."

"She genuinely believes things are going to work out in her favor, and it's crazy how often they actually do." Ben shook his head, grinning. "Call it luck. Call it manifesting. Call it whatever, but being around your sister made me want some of it. She's been trying to get through my thick skull for the past few years. Little by little, she's reprogramming me. Sometimes I straight up revert to my doomsday plotting, but I think for the most part, I'm more positive now than I was before. And I swear my quality of life is better for it."

"Did Maya put you up to this? Did she tell you to share that story with me?"

Ben shook his head, his brows coming together in confusion. "No. Why?"

"Oh. Because I've been going through some stuff, which I guess she has shared a bit with you, and I told her I want her to teach me how to approach life the way she does."

"I highly recommend it."

"I don't know," Katie groaned. "It's like I want that, but at the same time, I am who I am and I think how I think. You know?"

"Oh, I do know. Trust me. But you just need to make a conscious choice to think differently. What if for the next week while we're on this ship, you just assume everything is going to go well? The weather will be great, the food will be delicious, and you're going to have the time of your life. Every single morning, wake up and say, *Today is going to be a great day*. And then believe it's true and expect it to happen."

"But then what if it's not a great day?"

"Then you deal with it, same as you normally would. But what if it is? What if it is a great day, and you didn't waste any time you could be enjoying it by expecting it not to be?"

"So, should we be saying that your family is going to be fabulous, and they'll be really nice to me?"

"Ha," Ben scoffed. "I said we were going to think positively, not completely suspend reality."

"Oh, so you think positively about everything else, but

you're still dug into the trenches with this. Shouldn't it apply to your family as well?"

He thought about her words for a moment, and then a slow grin spread across his face. "Okay. All right. Touché. You called me out, and you're right. Maya would tell you I'm a work in progress. I'm still learning. So, what do you say we hold each other accountable this week? You work on believing it's going to be a great trip..."

"And you'll work on believing you're going to enjoy your family's company?"

"Whew," Ben exhaled with a soft laugh. "That's a big ask. *Enjoy their company*? How about we start with *there won't be any blow-ups*, or maybe *no one will storm out of a room angry*, or we could go with *no one will say anything that makes me want to punch something*?"

"Whichever one works best for you. Okay? Deal?" She offered her hand for him to shake, and then she stated her affirmations in an exaggerated upbeat voice. "This is going to be a great cruise. The weather will be perfect. The food will be divine. And I am going to have the time of my life."

"Aye, aye, matey!"

They turned the corner in the hallway to see a large backdrop featuring a rendering of the ship framed on either side by palm trees. A photographer stood by a camera on a stand, waving them over.

"Would you like a welcome photo, folks?"

Ben looked to Katie with an arched eyebrow. "Do you want to take a picture to document this moment?"

"Sure!" Katie followed the photographer's instructions and dropped her carry-on bag and her purse onto a chair by the camera stand, and then she walked forward toward the backdrop. When she turned, she realized Ben hadn't joined her and was instead waiting behind the photographer.

"You're not going to be in it?" the man asked as he looked over his shoulder at Ben.

"No," Ben said with a slight shake of his head. "I'll let the lady star in her own picture."

"What?" Katie motioned for him to join her. "No way. C'mon. Get over here."

"Are you sure?" he asked, and when she nodded and waved him over again, he walked toward her with his hands in his pockets. "Wouldn't you rather have one by yourself?"

"What? No. Why would I want a picture of me by myself? We're doing this cruise together, aren't we? We made a deal."

"Yeah, I guess we did." Ben smiled as he stepped into place beside her.

"Unless you don't want to?" Katie said, her eyes wide as she considered that his reluctance might not be strictly consideration of her feelings. "You don't have to. If you'd rather not be in the picture—"

"Don't be ridiculous," Ben said, wrapping his arm loosely around her shoulders as he faced the camera. "I'd love to be in the picture with you. Are you kidding me? I thought you'd never ask."

"A little closer," the photographer said. "Happy smiles."

Katie slid her arm around Ben's waist and stepped in closer, marveling at how solid he was. With his muscular arm encircling her shoulders and the faint hint of his cologne tickling her nose, she couldn't help wondering what it might be like to be in his embrace.

What if they really were a couple, and they were about to embark on an exciting adventure together? An anniversary trip, perhaps? Or maybe even their honeymoon? Or was a tropical getaway just something they did regularly?

She let her mind wander through various scenarios, and

then suddenly, the photographer was saying, "Okay, thanks. Have a great cruise."

She stepped away from Ben quickly, embarrassed to realize she'd been so lost in her imaginary life that she'd missed the real-life moment. She didn't even know if she'd smiled, but based on what she'd been thinking, she was certain she must have.

"Ready to get this party started?" Ben asked as he gathered her bags, handing her the purse and slinging her tote bag over his shoulder. "Man, this thing is heavy. What do you have in here? An anchor?"

"I can get it," she said, reaching for it, but Ben leaned slightly away and started walking.

"I got it. You have the other bag to carry. I have nothing."

They fell into step beside each other, and Katie found it hard to shake the micro-fantasies she'd been pursuing in her head.

It would have been nice if her very first vacation and her very first cruise could have been with a lover instead of someone she barely knew and had no connection with. Everything about the experience would hit differently viewed through a romantic lens.

She couldn't picture doing such a thing with Grant. He would have rushed her past the cheesy photo backdrop, but then again, he wouldn't have been boarding a cruise at all. He never traveled strictly for leisure. There always had to be a business angle involved.

But she could see herself doing this with someone she loved.

Someday.

When there was a someone.

"You still have your ID card out?" Ben asked as they

approached the short line of people ahead of them waiting at the threshold to board the ship. "They'll scan it to register that you're coming onto the ship, and then anytime you get off and get back on at a port, they scan it both ways. That way they can track whether you're on or off, and they know when everyone is back on board."

"But how do they know it's me holding the card?"

"Remember they took the picture at the check-in desk? It comes up when they scan your card."

He nudged her to move forward as they reached the podium and the crew member held his hand out for her card.

"Welcome aboard," the woman in the uniform said with a broad smile, which Katie promptly returned.

"That's me," Katie said to Ben and the crew member when she saw her smiling face on the screen, but then she added in a whisper to herself, "The new, adventurous, positive me."

They moved past the podium as she tucked the ID card into the outside pocket of her purse, and then she stopped to stare in awe at the multi-level openness of the ship's grand atrium.

"Beautiful, isn't it?" Ben said beside her.

"It's so...big. So open. I knew from the outside the ship was huge, and I'd seen pictures of this room online, but it's far grander than I imagined it to be. Are the steps on that staircase made of crystals?"

"Yeah. Looks like some shops up on that next level, and some kind of bar or lounge on the one above it."

"Yeah, I remember seeing those on the deck plans on the website. I made a list of everything I want to visit. Oh, wow!" she exclaimed as they entered the long main gallery, which was two stories high and lined on either side with restaurants and shops on both levels.

High above them, the arched ceiling was a beautiful myriad of panels that looked like stained glass windows stretching along the entire expanse of the gallery. But as Katie gazed up at the ceiling in amazement, the images shifted to a blue sky with clouds and balloons.

"Oh my gosh!" She slapped absent-mindedly against Ben's arm as she stumbled along looking up. "Did you see that?"

"Yeah." Ben laughed as he put his hand beneath her elbow to gently guide her around a group of people who had stopped to talk. "They're projections. They'll change throughout the cruise."

Turning her attention back to her immediate surroundings, she grabbed hold of his arm and stopped, pointing toward the shop on the right. Inside, display cases were filled with truffles of every color and variety as well as fudge in a plethora of flavors. "Look at all that chocolate! Can we take a closer look?"

"Of course." Ben steered them toward the chocolate shop, and Katie stopped in front of a large glass display case by the entrance. It held an intricate sculpture as tall as Katie featuring a compass centered inside a sun that was surrounded by waves. "Looks like the whole thing is carved out of chocolate. Oh, look at that one. It's a dragon."

"That's incredible!" Katie darted over to the next case to take a closer look at the dragon, and then she looked toward the counter and frowned. "They're not open. We can't buy any chocolate?"

"The shops are only open during certain hours, and never when we're in port. Something about duty taxes or sales restrictions from the local governments, I believe."

"Oh, that's right," Katie said, still crestfallen. "I do remember seeing something about that on the website."

"But we can come back when they're open and get chocolate," Ben offered. "For now, let's head to our room and put down the anchor you've got in this bag, and then we can do some exploring."

He'd called it *their* room, and though that was what it was, the word choice was jarring. She'd been coasting along in some sort of la-la land that was half amazement at what she was seeing and half fantasy of what she'd been imagining, and the reminder that she and Ben would be sharing a room brought her abruptly back to reality.

Suddenly conscious of how casually she'd been touching his arm as they'd taken in the sights, she shifted to put a bit more distance between them.

No matter what she might have imagined or what she might rather have, she and Ben were not a couple. They weren't even pretending to be one like he and Maya would have been. They were strangers, brought together by a series of odd circumstances.

SEVEN

Two more families crowded into the elevator with them, and Katie had to step closer to Ben to make room. She stood stiffly, trying to make sure no part of her body was touching his, but she felt his proximity all over.

She'd first been worried that sharing a room with Ben would be awkward because they didn't know each other. But in the short time she'd been around him, she's started to worry it would be difficult for entirely different reasons. Grant had been gone a long time, after all. Katie was human, and Ben was hot!

"Are you hungry?" he asked, and she jumped, a little startled that perhaps he had read her mind. But then, the more realistic explanation hit her.

"A little," she said, her cheeks filled with the warmth of embarrassment. "I think staring at that chocolate got my stomach primed, but I can wait if you're not ready to eat yet or if you wanted to go see your family first."

"No, we're good. I told Dad we'd probably get settled and maybe get some lunch, and then meet up."

"And they're okay with that?"

The corner of Ben's mouth lifted in a smirk. "They're fine with it. They have Brady to keep them entertained. They're not missing me."

"I'm sure that's not true," Katie said, and Ben sighed with a look that said he didn't agree.

She felt a ripple of anxiety when she thought about meeting Ben's mother. Surely, the woman couldn't be as awful as he'd made it sound. Maybe his rocky relationship with her had skewed his perception toward the negative, the same way she and Maya saw their mother as terribly annoying while everyone else thought she was sweet as pie.

But even if Lydia was every bit as terrible as Ben said, would she really be rude to someone she just met? Someone she didn't even know?

It was one thing to have animosity within the dynamics of the family, but why would she extend that to one of Ben's friends? Would this woman automatically dislike her right from the get-go just because she was with Ben? If so, that was messed up.

Maya had decided to be an obnoxious character because she assumed his family wouldn't like her and wouldn't be nice to her. She'd planned to stand her ground and give it back to them as good as she got. And that probably would have worked for Maya. She didn't typically care what people thought of her anyway.

Katie, on the other hand, had always been more of a people pleaser—the perpetual *nice girl*. The one all her friends' parents told them to be like. The teacher's pet. The boss's go-to.

And now she was about to meet people who had likely already made up their minds about her before they even met.

It doesn't matter whether Ben's family likes me, Katie told herself. *I will never see them again after this week.*

But wouldn't the week go much better for everyone involved if they did like her?

Surely, she could find a way to charm this woman. Maybe if she went with the opposite approach to Maya, she could find Lydia's good side and get on it. Katie's grandmother had always told her you have to catch bees with honey not vinegar, and though she'd thought that was ridiculously obvious as a child, she understood it on a different level as an adult.

From what she'd been told so far, it seemed to be important to Lydia for Ben to be in a relationship, and Katie wanted to think that was because any mother would want to see their child in a good place.

Perhaps if his mom thought he was happily attached, she might let up on him a bit. She might even welcome Katie if it seemed Ben was content with her.

Would they show her—and Ben—more respect if they believed he cared for her, and she for him? And could the two of them pull off pretending that they did?

She felt a familiar surge of adrenaline at the thought of conquering a challenge—of setting a goal and achieving it. It felt good to have a mission again. And as she'd done with every other mountain she'd decided to climb, she began to look for any hazards to be addressed and ways to improve her ascent.

Once they were off the elevator and alone, she asked, "What did you tell them about Maya? Like, did they know she was the one coming? Will they think it's weird that I'm not her?"

"No. In the initial conversation with my mother, I had

no idea who I was bringing, just that I needed to find someone so she didn't invite Allison."

"My grandmother used to get us confused all the time, so I could probably answer to *Maya* if I needed to."

"That would just be weird, and I wouldn't ask you to do that. But they don't know anything about Maya, so it won't be necessary."

"Did you tell your mom you were bringing a friend or a girlfriend?"

"I know I wouldn't have said it was a girlfriend since I didn't have one at the time. So, I'm fairly certain I said I was bringing a friend. But maybe I said *someone* and didn't specify any status. Can I ask why the word choice is so important?"

"Because if you didn't say *friend* specifically, your mom probably assumed you meant a romantic someone, right? I mean, isn't that why Maya opted to play that role instead of just coming as herself? As your friend?"

"You of all people should know there's no telling why Maya does what she does." Ben laughed as he rubbed his hand across the back of his neck. "She just announced she was coming along and that she would play the part of my girlfriend, as if there had been auditions and she'd won the role or something. And I can't speak to what my mother would assume. What I can tell you is it's not something you need to worry about. Really. It'll be fine."

He turned and continued down the passageway., but Katie wasn't finished. "But if you had to guess, your family is likely expecting me to be more of a girlfriend than a friend. Wouldn't you say?"

"Not necessarily. I've gone on trips with friends before."

"I'm sure. But how many cruises have you been on with

one single female friend where the two of you shared a room? You don't have to answer that, by the way. It's none of my business. I mention it only to prove my point."

Ben stopped again, fixing his gaze on hers as he crossed his arms and grinned. "I'm beginning to wonder what that point is. I assume you'll be getting to it soon?"

"Your mom wanted you to bring someone, right? When she thought you didn't have anyone lined up, she saw that as an opportunity to invite Allison. But then you said you were bringing someone after all. Don't you think she'd expect that person to be a romantic interest?"

"It's possible." His eyes narrowed beneath his furrowed brow. "I'm still not following why it matters."

"From what you've told me, your mom obviously wants you to be in a relationship. If you'd said you were involved with someone and would be bringing them right off the bat, she probably wouldn't have mentioned inviting Allison. Am I right?"

He titled his head from side to side, his lips twisted as he considered his answer. "I, uh, maybe. Probably. So, what are you saying?"

"I'm saying that I think Maya had the wrong approach. Well, maybe it was the right approach for Maya, but for me...for us...maybe we should go in the opposite direction. What if we try to convince your mom that you're dating someone and that you're happy? That might give her hope that you've finally settled down, which might, in turn, allow her to enjoy her cruise more, and then you and I can both enjoy our cruise as well."

Ben blinked a couple of times as he processed her words. "Wait a minute. Are you saying you've decided that now you want to pretend to be my girlfriend?"

Katie crossed her arms as well. "Well, I wouldn't say it's

necessarily something I *want* to do, but if there's a chance it would help make the trip a better experience for everyone, I'm willing to try it."

He stood staring at her without speaking, and the awkward silence made her rush to fill in the void.

"Unless you're just not feeling it, and that's fine. I know it was different with Maya since you guys are friends, and you don't know me from Adam, so you might not be able to pretend that we're, you know, close."

"That's not it. Not at all. I want to be clear when I tell you that I would be honored to have you as my girlfriend."

"*Pretend* girlfriend," Katie said with an exaggerated emphasis.

"Yes, of course. *Pretend* girlfriend. It's not that I have any issue with you, not at all. I'm just not sure it would have the effect on my mom that you think it would. Plus, you already told me you weren't comfortable with it, and you told Maya the same thing. You even just said it's not something you want to do, and I would never ask you to do something that made you uncomfortable. So why are we even having this conversation?"

She opened her mouth to answer, but Ben had turned to hold the key card against the lock pad on the door next to them, which meant this was *their* door to *their* room. With that realization, her curiosity shoved any response to the back of her mind, and the conversation was momentarily forgotten as she tried to see through the open door past Ben.

Her first thought was that the room seemed smaller than it had looked in the website pictures, but she wondered if maybe that was because Ben's large frame was filling the narrow entryway, and his head almost reached the ceiling.

Once he moved forward enough for her to get a good look at the entire room, her concern about its size paled in comparison to her alarm about the king-sized bed that dominated the space.

"I thought you said there would be separate beds."

"It was supposed to be two twins. That's what I requested. I'll talk to the room steward. Maybe this is one of those rooms where the king converts into two twins. Or there's probably a sofa bed or a bunk that comes out of the ceiling or something. We'll work it out, somehow. I promise."

Nodding, she moved further into the room, setting her purse on the small table in front of the sofa. Pushing the sleeping arrangements aside for the moment, she continued her exploration of the room. Her excitement returned as she checked out the bathroom vanity and shower and opened each of the closet doors and the drawers inside the closet.

She was back to grinning from ear to ear as she ran to the sliding glass door and pulled it open to step out onto the balcony.

"Oh, wow. This is great."

Ben stepped out beside her, his gaze scanning the port. "This is nothing. Wait until the view is the sun setting over the water. Or the white caps frothing up in the midnight sea under the reflection of the moon."

A chill ran over Katie at the prospect of either, and she hugged herself, once again tickled beyond belief at her good fortune in landing this trip. "If we leave the door open at night, can we hear the waves?"

"Yes, but the AC system is designed to shut off when the door's open so the ship isn't working to cool the entire atmosphere. It might get stuffy, but we can certainly try it."

She grinned, hugging herself tighter. "When Maya and I were little, my parents would take us to the beach for a week every summer, and I always loved falling asleep to the sound of the waves through the open balcony door."

"You'll hear the water, for sure, but it's not the same as waves crashing onto the beach. It's still soothing though, and the boat will rock you to sleep."

"That sounds wonderful."

"Ready to go see more of the ship and get something to eat?"

She nodded, her grin as wide as could be as she looked up at him. In that moment, she could understand why Maya urged her to focus on the present.

Beyond that balcony, all the problems of the world and the uncertainty of her future still existed, and beyond the door of their stateroom, the issues with his family awaited.

But right then, right there, everything was beautiful. A handsome and kind man was staring down at her with a smile so big his chocolate brown eyes were alight with it. The sky was the most brilliant blue imaginable, without a cloud in sight. Tidbits of laughter and joyful conversations drifted through the air from somewhere above them on the ship, and a pair of seagulls flew by, cawing to one another in a language all their own.

Having found such happiness in that one moment, Katie thought perhaps she could believe there was more of it to come.

EIGHT

A s they made their way up to the restaurant on the Lido Deck, Ben insisted on a detour to the uppermost deck so Katie could see the horizon in all directions. She giggled as she looked over the railing to the water several stories below, and then she pointed toward the rear of the ship, where she'd spotted a somewhat secluded pool and hot tub.

Along their way to take a closer look, they found the basketball court, the bowling alley, the runner's track, the arcade, and the shuffleboard court.

With each new revelation, Katie became more astounded by the sheer size of the ship and how much there was to do.

"It really is like a floating city," she said as they stood at a railing and gazed down at the main pool and the people swimming or milling about on lounge chairs, at bars, or seated at tables surrounding the pool.

"I'd say a big resort hotel that happens to be on the water but has all the same amenities one would have on land."

"I've never been to a resort this big," Katie said.

"You have now."

They filled up at the Lido buffet, and once they'd finished, Ben texted his dad to find out their whereabouts.

"They're at a lounge on Deck 5, Midship, and they're ready to meet up if we are."

Katie watched the tension creep into his face, tightening his jaw as the light in his eyes dulled, and his ever-present grin faded.

"Boy, they really get to you, don't they? And I thought I had it bad with stressing out about my mom."

"I'm okay." He shrugged as though it was no big deal, but the gesture was less than convincing. "I'm used to it. I just want them to be nice to you."

"Well, I plan to be nice to them, so if they're not...like I said before...that's on them. Not on you."

"Right. Okay." He leaned forward, his eyes somber as they searched hers. "This is your last chance to back out."

Neither of them had mentioned her idea since she'd first suggested it in the hallway and he'd ended the conversation. She'd assumed it was a no-go, but had he decided to give it a try?

"What do you mean by *back out*?"

"I mean this is your last chance to change your mind."

"About what? Meeting your parents? Or telling them we're involved as more than just friends?"

With a grin that was half-smirk, he said, "Both, I suppose. If you've decided you don't want to meet them at all, I'd understand."

"So, then were you saying you do want to try my plan?"

He bit down on his lip, shaking his head slowly as though he was still struggling with the decision. "The way you laid it out made sense, but like I said before, I don't know that it will charm my mother the way you hope it will. This thing with her and me, it's complicated. Scheming to win her favor could blow up in our faces, and the last thing I want is for you to be collateral damage because of me."

"I thought we committed to think positively and expect the best outcome while we're on this trip." She smiled at him, and then she smiled up at the young man who had offered to clear their dishes. Once the man finished and departed, she leaned forward with her arms folded on the table. "I can't promise to be as convincing as Maya might have been, but I'll do my best. I'm in if you are. It's your family, so it must be your decision."

"Yeah, and that means I'll be responsible for whatever happens. Let's go. I've kept them waiting long enough."

"Okay, but what are we doing? Are we dating or not?"

"I don't know. I'll decide on the way over. C'mon."

Gone was the charming tour guide he'd been before, and as she followed a silent and broody Ben to the lounge on Deck 5, the change in his mood caused her anxiety to escalate.

This was crazy. There was no way she could lie to his family. She'd never pull it off. As a teenager, she'd tried to lie to her mother once, and that had ended horribly. She'd convinced Rosalyn she was going to a study group at a friend's house, but on the drive over, she'd burst into tears out of guilt and confessed it was really a party.

So, as much as she wanted to help Ben, and as bad as she felt about how his family messed with his head, it would only make things worse for him if she screwed up and they determined they'd been lied to.

No, they needed to just stick with Plan A and tell everyone they were friends. Which was still a lie. Not counting the concert she didn't remember, they'd only just met that morning. They weren't friends. Not yet, anyway. But based on what she'd learned of him in the short time they'd been talking, and based on how Maya already felt about him, she was certain they would be friends in time.

So that was an easier lie to pull off.

"Hey, hold up a minute," she said, laying her hand on his arm as she paused in the hallway outside the lounge. "Let's forget about the whole girlfriend scheme. You're probably right. It's a bad idea, and it could totally blow up in our faces. I've never been that good of an actress, and I am a terrible liar. I don't want to make things worse for you."

"Okay." Ben smiled, giving her a single nod. "Then that settles it. I'll tell them we met about a year ago through your sister, who's a close friend, and that we recently reconnected. We discovered we enjoy each other's company and became fast friends. Friendly enough that we decided to travel together. Is that close enough to the truth?"

"Um, yeah. For sure. Thanks."

"No problem." He gave her upper arm a light squeeze of reassurance. "Don't worry. It's gonna be great."

"Yes. It is," she said in a confident voice she hoped would reassure them both.

Ben smiled, but there was something in his eyes that she couldn't decipher. Something that made her feel sad.

"Ready?" he asked, thumbing toward the lounge.

"Yeah." They started to walk again, but then she stopped him once more. "Oh, there's a restroom. Let me duck in and check the mirror. My hair's probably blown all over the place from when we were out in the wind, and even if we're just friends, I'd like to make a good first impression."

"You look great, but yeah, do whatever you need to do."

Katie walked behind the built-in partition in front of the ladies' room door, stepping aside so the woman exiting could pass. Once in the restroom, she ran her fingers through her hair, straightening it as best as she could, and then she brushed on a bit of lip gloss.

She'd just opened the door to exit when she heard a woman exclaim, "Benjamin! There you are. We thought you'd gotten lost. All the hallways on this godforsaken ship look the same. Where's your friend?"

Katie paused, steeling herself for the moment she'd been dreading. What was the best approach? Should she say hello and introduce herself or wait for Ben to make the introductions? She wished she'd thought to ask him if Lydia was a handshaker, a hugger, or a hands-off person who preferred no contact when first meeting someone.

"She's in the restroom," Ben said as Katie stood hidden behind the partition determining her plan of action.

"Not powdering her nose, I hope." Lydia said in a nasally tone.

"Why would you even say that?"

"Well, you do have a history of choosing poorly when it comes to women and addicts, do you not?"

Katie had just started to emerge from behind the partition, but the shock of that question stopped her in her tracks.

"She's definitely not an addict," Ben said, the frustration obvious in his voice. "But hey, thanks for bringing that up within the first five minutes of seeing me. I was nineteen. I didn't know any better."

"Please. You knew better. You dated her to embarrass me. And you weren't nineteen the other time, were you? So, who's this one? Where did you find her?"

"This one is different, and I would really appreciate if you could at least try to be nice to her."

"Different? Different, how?"

"I'm serious. I'm really interested in this girl, and I don't need you causing any problems for me."

Katie's brows lifted in surprise. What was he doing? Had he changed his mind and decided to say they were dating? But they'd just agreed to go with the truth. Crap! Now that he'd said it, she had to go with it. She had to back him up. But how? She hadn't met a boyfriend's mom since high school. She was sorely out of practice.

"Benjamin, what problems could I possibly cause?" Lydia asked, her voice sickeningly sweet. "And you can't be that interested in her if you've never brought her home to meet your family."

"You're meeting her now."

"You've told us nothing about her. Not even a mention other than a vague comment that you'd be bringing a friend. You certainly never called Allison a friend. She says hello, by the way. Your father and I had her over for dinner before we left. She's doing well."

Okay, time to act, Katie thought.

What would a normal person do when meeting their boyfriend's mother for the first time?

Or better yet, what would Maya do?

That one was at least easy to answer.

Stepping out from the partition, Katie strode over to Ben with all the confidence she knew her sister would exude.

"Hey, babe. Sorry it took me so long." Without taking too much time to think, she just acted on impulse the way she thought Maya would, cupping Ben's face in her hands as she pressed her lips to his.

He froze, momentarily stunned, but then his arms were around her, and his hands were in her hair, and suddenly, she wasn't sure who was kissing who.

"Excuse me," Lydia said. "I'm standing right here."

Ben released Katie from the kiss but kept her in his arms.

"Sorry. Um, Mother, this is Kate. Kate, my mother, Lydia."

"Oh my goodness," Katie managed to say, even though she was unexpectedly dizzy from the kiss. "I've heard so much about you."

She knew instinctively that Lydia Reyes was definitely not a hugger, and though she honestly thought the correct answer was no-contact, she offered a handshake so as not to appear rude.

"Have you now?" Lydia accepted the handshake offer but lifted her chin to peer down her nose at Katie, who was shorter by at least three inches. "I've heard absolutely nothing about you."

Wow. This lady was a piece of work. This was going to be a challenge, for sure, and Katie had always excelled at challenges.

"Hey—" Ben said to his mother in reproach, but Katie laid her hand on his chest to quiet him.

"That's my fault," she said, keeping her voice chipper and light. "I told Ben I wasn't comfortable with him telling people that we were dating. I didn't want to jinx things. I thought it would be best if we got to know one another without the pressure of a label or other people's expectations. But I am thrilled to finally meet you and to tell you how wonderful your son is. But of course, you already know that."

She'd tried to stick to the truth as much as possible,

which she'd always heard was a technique the best liars do to keep track of the story. It was also what Maya did when they were growing up, and it had worked for her most of the time.

Lydia smiled, but her eyes remained cold and serious. "Come. Let me introduce you to the rest of the family. They've been very curious to know who Ben was bringing."

What was that? Ben mouthed to her as they followed his mother inside the lounge.

Katie didn't dare answer out loud and risk Lydia hearing, so she just shrugged. Had he not expected her to follow his lead? Had she misread the situation somehow? Or was the kiss maybe a step too far?

He definitely didn't seem to mind it at the time, but now that the adrenaline of the moment had passed, she wondered if perhaps it had been a bit much on her part. Maybe in hindsight she should have just walked out and said hello.

Yeah, that was probably what the normal person would have done.

That's what old Katie would have done, for sure.

But this was new, adventurous Katie. She took matters in her own hands. Literally.

NINE

"Look who I found in the hall," Lydia said to the table of people they were approaching. Her voice was much kinder than it had been outside, as though she'd flipped on a switch.

"Uncle Ben!" Brady shouted in a flash of navy and red as he ran into Ben's arms.

"Hey, Braidster!" Ben tossed him above his head, laughing, and Brady's giggles filled the air.

"Ben," admonished a tall, slender woman who looked so much like her brother that Katie knew at once she was Laura. "Don't toss him like that. His tummy is full of lunch and you're going to make him sick. Not to mention that you might drop him."

"I'm not going to drop the Braidster," Ben said as he held Brady to him with his muscular arms wrapped securely around the child's hips. Suddenly, Ben's mouth popped open in a breathy "O" as he teased his nephew by releasing him for a split second and then catching him again. He did it several times in quick succession, with Brady squealing louder each time he was dropped.

"Brady, stop squealing," Laura said. "Ben, you're getting him all riled up."

"This is Ben's *friend*, Kate," Lydia said to the group, lingering a little extra on the label.

"Uh, it's Katie actually," Katie said as she lifted her hand in greeting. "Only my sister calls me Kate."

Lydia's brows rose. "I could have sworn my son just introduced you as Kate. Did I hear him incorrectly?"

"And Ben," Katie added awkwardly as she made eye contact with him over Brady's head. "Ben calls me Kate."

The gray-haired gentleman stood and shook her hand, introducing himself as Ben's dad, Martin. "You'd like us to call you Katie?"

"Uh, Kate is fine," Katie said, despite protesting the name all her life.

Ben stepped forward to stand beside her. "She prefers Katie."

She was surprised to hear him speak up for her. They'd never had a conversation regarding her preference for her name. In fact, she couldn't remember ever hearing Ben say her name.

"I met Katie through her sister, who's a close friend, so I was introduced to her as Kate, and the name kind of stuck. I need to work harder at unlearning it."

Katie sent him an appreciative glance as he stepped forward to hug his father, and then she turned her focus to Ben's sister, who was now standing and watching her alongside a tall blond gentleman.

"I'm Laura," she said, "Ben's sister, and this is my husband, Dale. That's our son, Brady. It's nice to meet you. We live so far away we rarely get to meet any of Ben's friends."

"Where do you live?" Katie asked, and then she realized that was probably an answer Ben's girlfriend should know.

"In a small town in Northern California. I doubt you've heard of it. We lived here in Miami for a while, but we moved back home to be closer to Mom and Dad after Brady was born. Brady, can you say hello to Uncle Ben's friend?"

"Are you his girlfriend? Do you kiss him on the mouth?" Brady asked, and Ben laughed as his sister chastised her son.

"Brady! That's rude. Where on earth did you come up with such a thing? You need to apologize now. Say you're sorry to Kate...er, Katie."

"He's fine," Katie said. "He doesn't have to apologize."

"Yes, he does," Laura insisted. "Brady, apologize now."

"I'm sorry," Brady said, his smile gone and his entire demeanor so crestfallen Katie couldn't help but feel sorry for him.

"It's okay," she told him.

"I'm curious to hear the answer to the question," said Dale with a leering grin. "The first one. The second one I can guess."

"The answer is yes," Ben said as he set Brady back on the ground. "Katie has officially taken me off the market."

He put his arm around her waist, and the sudden closeness sent a ripple of gooseflesh skittering across her skin.

The peal of electronic chimes filled the air, and a man with an Italian accent introduced himself over the PA system before instructing all passengers to return to their room for the muster drill procedure.

"That's the safety video thing, right?" Katie said to Ben. "I read we have to watch it and then check in somewhere."

Brady turned to Laura. "Do we have to do that?"

Laura squatted in front of him, tucking her thumb beneath his chin. "Yes, everyone must do it. We've done it before, remember? They teach us how to get to the lifeboats in case the ship was to sink. That's why you need to stay with Mommy and Daddy all the time, so that if something happens and the ship does start to sink, we'll be able to get in the lifeboat together."

"Christ, Laura," Dale said, scowling. "Way to terrify the kid. This ship isn't going to sink, buddy."

"That's what the passengers on the Titanic said." Martin laughed at his own sick joke, but he was the only one of the group who did.

Laura took Brady's hand and then nudged Dale. "We should go."

Dale sat back down in his chair as he held his glass up toward his wife. "I haven't finished my drink. I'm not going anywhere until I do."

Laura frowned and put her hand on her hip. "They're trying to clear the lounge, and the longer we stay, the crazier the elevators are going to get. Brady can't do nine flights of stairs, Dale."

"By the time I finish my drink, most of these people will be back in their rooms and the elevators will be fine."

"Yes, but then everyone would be waiting for us. They can't end the muster drill until everyone has watched the video and checked in at their station. You know that."

Dale's eyes were hard as he stared at his wife. "I'm going to sit here and finish my drink, and no one is going to rush me. If you want to go, go."

"C'mon," Ben said to Katie, and the two of them followed Martin and Lydia out of the lounge with Laura and Brady close behind.

Martin clapped Ben on the shoulder as the group

walked toward the elevators. "It's nice to see you, son. I'm glad you could make it. Things still going well in Barcelona?"

"Yes, sir. Very well. I sold another sculpture this week."

"That's good, that's good. You keep doing your thing." Martin's wide grin was similar to his son's, and Katie realized Ben and Laura both took after their father more than their mother. "Katie, we didn't get to talk much with this muster business, but we'll see the two of you for dinner, no?"

"Yeah, we'll be there," Ben responded. "Six-thirty, right?"

Lydia leaned forward to look at her son. "You should be there at six-ten. The closer it gets to the seating time, the more crowded it is at the doors. And please do dress appropriately."

Katie hadn't realized the last comment was directed to her until she noticed Lydia giving a once-over, allowing her fierce gaze to drift down Katie's body.

The disdain evident in the appraisal left Katie feeling exposed, even though the sundress she wore came to her knees and covered her breasts completely, leaving only her shoulders and arms bare. Still, she was tempted to cross her arms over her chest to hide from Lydia's scrutiny, but before she could give in to the urge, Ben put his arm around her in what felt like a protective move.

"We know how to dress, Mother."

"I was just trying to be helpful, dear. Based on her comment about the muster drill, she clearly hasn't cruised before."

Ben's arm tightened around her ever so slightly. "No, but we've both eaten in restaurants, and not surprisingly, the dress code at sea is much the same."

An elevator opened, but it already had several people inside it, so Ben motioned for his family to go ahead.

"You guys take this one. We'll wait for the next one."

To her surprise, he didn't move his arm from her shoulders once his family had gone, and to her even greater surprise, she didn't either. It felt nice. Comfortable. Close.

It was only seconds before another elevator opened, and since this one was less crowded, Ben stepped forward and held the door with his hand so she could enter.

"All things considered, I think that went pretty well," Katie said once they'd exited the elevator and were alone. "Wouldn't you say?"

Ben stopped and turned to stare at her, his eyes wide and his brows high on his forehead. "What was with that kiss? I mean, I'm not complaining, not one single iota, but I sure didn't see that coming."

Katie flushed hot with the memory of the kiss and the embarrassment of his questioning. "I was following your signal, your lead. What made you change your mind?"

"What are you talking about? What signal?"

"When I came out of the bathroom, you were telling your mother you were interested in me and asking her to be nice. I figured you must have changed your mind and decided to go with Plan B—trying to convince her you're in a relationship and happy."

"Oh, I was definitely happy in that moment."

"But that's what you were doing, right?" Katie crossed her arms and shrank into herself a bit as she began to suspect that she might have screwed up. "You were setting up the ruse? Please tell me I didn't totally misread the situation and kiss you out of nowhere for no reason."

"No, you're good. And hey, even if you had, it was worth it. That was some kiss!"

He grinned as he headed toward their room, and Katie laughed as she followed him with a mixture of relief and bashfulness, wishing the memory of the kiss didn't still make her lips tingle.

What if they needed to kiss again before the week was through? She wasn't opposed to the idea, but how would she explain to her ridiculously overreactive body that it was all pretend?

"Hey, and I'm sorry about the Kate thing," Ben said as they continued down the passageway toward their room. "That's what I've always heard Maya call you, so I guess I assumed it was your name. I should have paid better attention. I'll work on calling you Katie from now on."

"We've already told your family that you call me Kate, so you might as well keep doing it. It's okay. I don't hate the variation. I've just always preferred Katie. Which is probably why Maya started calling me Kate when we were young, but honestly, it was so long ago, I don't even remember why she started. But it stuck. To her, I'm Kate. And to you, I suppose. I noticed your mother calls you Benjamin."

"Or Benjamin David, if she's mad."

"She seemed...nice."

Ben cut his eyes toward her. "Pfft. No, she didn't, and you don't have to say that."

"We're supposed to be positive, remember?"

He unlocked their door and stepped aside so Katie could enter. "We may be lying to everyone else, but we need to stay honest with each other."

"We forgot to tell someone to make it twins," she said as she stared at the bed.

"No problem. I'll call the room steward. Turn on the TV so we can watch the safety video. Once it's done, they'll tell us a number to call to verify we've seen it, and then we'll have to go check in at our muster station."

She grabbed the remote to turn on the television while Ben called, but he got no answer.

"The stewards may be participating in the muster drill somehow. It's fine. We'll find someone before they do turndown."

They watched the safety video and checked in at their assigned station, and then the two of them went up on the highest deck for the sail-away celebration.

"We're moving," Katie said as she grabbed onto the rail, "but I don't feel us moving. I see that we're passing things, but I don't feel the movement."

"You might not feel it much the entire trip. Some are more sensitive to it than others. It rocks and sways more if the seas get rough or if the ship is in a hurry to be somewhere, but of the most part, the stabilizers do their job and it's smooth sailing."

Once the ship was underway, Ben nudged Katie with his elbow. "We probably should head back downstairs if you want to shower before dinner."

"Ah, I do, but I hate to leave this view."

"It's gonna be pretty much the same for the next few days except when we're in port. In the daytime, we're surrounded by beautiful turquoise blue water, and at night, we're surrounded by the deepest, darkest black you've ever seen."

"Can we come up back up here at night?"

"Of course."

They went back to the room, pleased to find their luggage had already arrived. After deciding who got which drawer and shelf, they began to unpack.

"I was thinking I'll hop in the shower first, if that's

okay," Ben said as he gathered his clothes for dinner. "I'll only be a few minutes, and then I can head out so you have the room to yourself to get ready."

"That would be great, thanks. I'll take a walk. How much time do you need?"

"Oh, I can get dressed in the bathroom. You don't have to go anywhere."

"Are you sure? I don't mind."

"It's up to you. If you want to take a walk, then by all means, you should. But if you'd rather hang out in here to finish unpacking, I'm fine changing in the bathroom."

He was done and dressed for dinner by the time she had everything put away, and at the sight of him in a black dress shirt and black dress pants with his hair still damp from the shower, she questioned her sanity for ever thinking this was a good idea.

"You look nice," she said, breathing in the clean, woodsy scent of his cologne as he rolled back the cuffs of his sleeves.

"Thank you. The water gets extremely hot very quickly, so be careful. I left the dial in a spot that was perfect for me, but I'm not sure how you like your water. I'm going to head out, but you should be able to message me through that ship app we downloaded onto your phone. Just buzz me when you're ready, and I can either meet you here or somewhere near the dining room."

"Got it. What about the beds?"

"Usually, the room steward comes by to introduce themselves, so I hope we didn't miss them when we were out exploring earlier. I'll try and track someone down, but if they happen to stop by while you're getting ready, just tell them we need separate sleeping arrangements. We can try to call again, too."

"Okay, I'll do that while you're gone, just in case you don't find them and they don't stop by."

She got ready as quickly as she could, not wanting to keep him waiting and not wanting to make them late to meet his parents.

The black dress was borrowed from Maya, and she'd loved it when she tried it on at home, but it hadn't seemed so short back then. It fit great, and it showcased her legs quite well, which was why she'd liked it at the time, but she feared Lydia might find it inappropriate.

With a swear beneath her breath, she went through the closet again to find an alternative, but with two nights being formal and two others being themed, her options for tonight were limited. All of them were short, which was evidently the only style of dress Maya wore.

As the clock marched closer to their meeting time for dinner, she finally decided that she wouldn't allow Lydia to determine her skirt length or what was appropriate for her.

The dress covered everything it should and was neither too revealing nor too tight. And though the skirt was a few inches above her knee, it was no more leg exposed than there would be in a swimsuit or a pair of short shorts.

After one more unsuccessful attempt to reach the room steward by phone, she grabbed the tiny black handbag she'd packed specifically to use at dinner, and then she headed up to meet Ben at a bar near the dining room.

Just as she had in the airport, she spotted him first, and she knew the moment he saw her. His eyes widened ever so slightly, and his lips parted, and all she could think about was the kiss they'd shared earlier.

"Hi," she said, tugging at the hemline of the skirt.

"You look incredible," Ben replied. "Wow. How on

earth did I get so lucky? I have the most beautiful pretend girlfriend in the world."

Katie grinned as she playfully tapped his arm with the handbag. "Well, you set the bar pretty high, so I had to rise to your level. Unfortunately, I think this skirt rose with me. Do you think it's too short?"

She tugged at the hemline again as she looked down at the skirt, and then she looked back up at Ben.

"You're asking me, a guy, if I think your little black dress is too short? C'mon. How do you expect me to answer that? It's like asking me to run through a minefield."

"I expect you to tell me the truth."

"The truth? Okay. I'm sure you realize that you have great legs, Kate. I mean, I know you have mirrors in your home, so you must. And that dress with those legs?" He whistled soft and low. "Perfection. I wouldn't change a thing."

"Thanks, now how about giving me an honest answer from your mother's point of view instead of a guy's? Is it too short to be appropriate for dinner?"

"Is that what this is about?" He rolled his eyes and swore. "Please don't let her rent space in your head. If you're comfortable wearing it, wear it. What she thinks should have no bearing on the decision. It doesn't matter."

"But it does matter. She's your mother. I want to make a good impression. I mean, you know, for the, uh, the pretending thing."

"The only opinion that should matter is your own. Do you like the dress?"

"Yeah," she said, looking down at it again. "It's Maya's, and I loved it when I put it on at home, but it didn't seem so short then."

"I don't know what you want me to say. The dress is

fine, and you look great in it. You look like a million bucks, and I bet you'll turn every head on this ship. But if you're uncomfortable and you're gonna be pulling at the skirt all night, then go change. I'll wait here. But do it for you, not because of my mother."

Katie bit down on her lip, smoothing her hands over the dress. She did know she had great legs. She'd always considered them her best physical feature. And she liked the way the dress fit. It had made her feel good the first time she tried it on, and she hated that she'd allowed Lydia to change that. Screw Lydia! Ben was right. His mother's opinion should have no bearing on what Katie wore.

She lifted her chin, squaring her shoulders as she smiled. "All right. Well, if I look like a million bucks, why on earth would I change?"

"My thoughts exactly." Ben motioned toward the menu card on the bar in front of him. "Would you like a drink before we head down to dinner?"

"Don't we need to get going? Your mom said to meet them at ten after."

"They don't open the dining room until six-thirty, so if we get down there at six-ten, we'll stand around and wait for twenty minutes with my family. I'd rather wait here at the bar. With you. So, I texted my dad that we'd be there when the dining room opens."

"Sounds good to me." She hoisted herself onto the barstool next to him, praying she didn't flash him in the process as the skirt rode up her thighs.

"What would you like?" Ben asked. "A glass of wine? A cocktail? A soda?"

"What are you having? It looks refreshing."

"Cranberry and seltzer, with a twist of lime. Would you like one?"

"Oh, I forgot. You did say you don't drink. Something else you have in common with my sister. Was that from her influence as well?"

"No. I had stopped drinking long before I met Maya."

"I remember now that she said you helped her when she and Louise broke up. Was it you that convinced her to stop drinking?"

He took a sip from his glass before answering. "I don't know that anyone can really convince another person to stop drinking. It's a decision they must make for themselves. But I tried to be there for Maya in whatever way I could when she was ready to make that choice."

"Thank you. I'm glad you were there for my sister and that she had someone like you to lean on."

"She's my friend," Ben said, shrugging one shoulder. "We lean on each other."

Ten

The rest of the family was already seated when Ben and Katie arrived at the restaurant, and she was relieved to see that neither of the open seats was next to Lydia. Given the choice between Martin and Laura for a seatmate, she went with Ben's sister to be farther away from his mom, but that placement put them face to face across the table from each other.

After everyone exchanged greetings and the drink and dinner orders were placed, Martin turned to Katie and began the inevitable getting-to-know-you interrogation.

"Tell us where you're from."

She and Ben had agreed they'd go with the truth whenever possible, so she smiled and answered easily. "Florida. I grew up in a small town called Cedar Creek about a half hour northwest of Orlando."

"Ah, a Florida native," Martin said. "I hear those aren't too common."

"My family has been in the state for several generations, but Florida does have a lot of transplants and part-time residents, so I can see why people think that."

"What do you do for a living?" Lydia asked, her manner brusquer than Martin's, so even though it was another easy answer as far as truth, Katie couldn't help feeling the stakes were higher.

"Um, I'm in a bit of a transition period right now, so I'm helping my sister out at her surf shop until I figure out what comes next."

"Kate's a writer," Ben offered, and she whipped her head around to look at him, wishing she could stop the words coming out of his mouth. "She was working for a publishing firm in New York, but she's taking some time off to work on her own novel now."

Where did that come from?

She hadn't told Ben any of that, so she could only assume it came from Maya. But why was he telling his family personal details about her life?

"A writer," Laura exclaimed. "How exciting!"

Dale leaned forward, looking at Katie with a new interest. "A writer, eh? What do you write? Anything I would have read?"

This line of questioning was like something out of Katie's own personal nightmares, where her greatest failure was being highlighted and pointed out to people who were sitting around waiting to judge her.

Her skin grew prickly and hot, and she shifted in her seat as they stared and waited for her answer. "Uh, no. I don't have anything published."

Crossing her arms, Lydia made a soft grunting noise and then tilted her head to the side with a sly grin. "You worked for a publisher and couldn't get them to publish you? What on earth do you write?"

Ouch. Lydia had gone straight for the jugular, and when

Katie opened her mouth to respond, no words would form on her tongue.

"She didn't work for the publisher in a writing capacity," Ben interjected. "She was in a different role."

"What's your book about?" Laura asked. Her eyes were bright, and her warm smile made Katie feel like she was genuinely interested in the answer.

Unfortunately, there was no answer to give. Because there was no book.

There should be one. In fact, there should have been several by now. But Katie hadn't been able to finish a story since college, and in the recent years, she couldn't even begin one.

She'd started to fear that maybe she wasn't a writer after all, and now, she feared that everyone at the table knew that.

"I, um, I haven't...it's just..."

"If it's a work in progress, she may not want to discuss it," said Martin. "I know lots of creatives who feel it jinxes the project to talk about it too soon."

"Well, if she's going to be successful as an author, at some point she'll need to be able to answer questions about her book." Lydia sat back in her chair and stared at Katie. "What genre is it?"

"If she doesn't want to discuss it, she doesn't have to," Ben said, his tone growing more defensive.

Katie wondered if it was in response to her obvious discomfort or if it was something between the two of them that had nothing to do with her.

Shifting her glare to her son, Lydia barked, "You're the one who brought it up."

"Yes, well, that's because I think it's very cool that she's writing a book, and I got a little carried away with my excitement and shared that with all of you. I should have left it up to Kate whether she wanted to discuss it."

Katie wanted to hug him and yell at him, all at the same time.

She was angry that he'd put her on the spot like that but relieved that he'd recognized it and tried to shut it down.

In a case of perfect timing, their waiter arrived at that moment to deliver the first course, temporarily shelving the subject of Katie's life and her writing.

Brady did his part throughout the meal to keep everyone entertained, but by the time the entree dishes had been cleared, the conversation returned to Katie.

"How did the two of you meet?" Laura asked, turning in her chair to devote her attention to Katie. "Give me all the details. I love a good love story."

The truth in this instance was a bit more complicated, since Katie didn't remember it happening.

"Ben and I met a little over a year ago at a concert while I was visiting my sister in Florida."

"And? That's it?" Laura groaned. "C'mon! You're a writer. Gimme the details. Who saw who first? What made you notice each other? How did that get to this?"

Katie had run out of truths to tell, and her palms were sweating with the pressure of creating a backstory filled with lies. Looking to Ben, she smiled sweetly and tossed him the grenade. "You tell this story so much better than I can, *honey*. Go ahead."

He grinned and took a sip of water before beginning.

"It was a beach concert, and we were with a large group of people. I saw Kate when she first arrived with her sister, and immediately, I started asking everyone who she was. I didn't really get to talk to her during the show—loud concerts aren't great for striking up a conversation—but afterward, a bunch of us went to this bar downtown, and I scored a seat at the table where she was sitting."

Katie frowned as she tried to recall that night. She'd been in such a funk over Grant moving to London that she hadn't been interested in the show or anyone attending it with them. She remembered the restaurant, but there were so many people gathered around that she found it hard to picture their faces.

How much of the tale he was spinning was truth and what was embellished to create their story? Obviously, the restaurant part was true, but had he really sat at her table? Had they talked? She couldn't believe she didn't remember him at all.

With her elbow on the table, she propped her chin in her hand, riveted to Ben's story and just as curious as anyone else to hear what happened next.

"Someone mentioned that Kate worked in publishing, and before long, that led to a spirited debate between her and my friend Paul on the merits of romance as a fiction genre. Paul was being a bit of a jerk."

That part Katie remembered, and she nodded in agreement with Ben's jerk assessment as he went on with his story.

"Paul wouldn't budge on his assertion that romance novels have inherently inferior plots. He said that disqualifies them as literature. He called them...what was it—"

"Bodice-rippers," Katie chimed in. "Ugh."

"That's it," Ben said. "Bodice-rippers. Paul said they're nothing but sex and fluff, but Kate laid out a thorough case for the number of different sub-genres within romance, each with its own complexities. She came at him armed with so much evidence that I wondered if she'd spent time in court. She knew her stuff, and she didn't back down from Paul, which was impressive. He can be intimidating. Even to those of us who call him a friend. But Kate just—"

"So, you write romance." Lydia cut Ben short with the conclusion she'd drawn, and her derisive tone left no doubt as to her opinion on the matter.

Ben bristled in response. "We're not discussing Katie's writing."

"Again, you chose the topic," Lydia said. "I was merely trying to learn more about your travel companion...since you've told us nothing regarding her."

"If you met a year ago, how long have you been dating?" Laura asked, either oblivious to the tension at the table or unbothered by it.

Katie looked at Ben for an answer, but then she remembered she'd insinuated to Lydia earlier that they were still in the beginning stage of their relationship. Concerned he might contradict that, she blurted out, "Six weeks."

At the same exact moment, Ben told them four months.

"Oh, has it been that long?" Katie let out a nervous laugh to try and cover for their mistake.

"Did you guys start dating at different times?" Martin asked, his accompanying laugh boisterous. "How can you not know when you got together?"

Ben looked at his dad and shrugged. "It just kind of happened. I don't think we have an official date on the calendar to mark the occasion. We started off as friends, but for me, at least, there was a spark right from the start. It didn't go anywhere for a long time, but I always had her on my mind, and I'd ask Kate's sister about her every now and then, just to check in. Then, lucky for me, we met again under different circumstances, and things have progressed rather quickly since then. I knew right away this was special, but I think the experience has been different for Kate. Right, *babe*?"

It took a second for Kate to process everything he'd said and determine how to answer. "Right. Yeah. He knew before I did. And as far as dates and times, I'm horrible with remembering stuff like that. I just let Ben keep track of everything."

She hoped he was keeping track of what they'd said so they didn't mess up and contradict themselves again. This was beyond nerve-wracking for her, especially when his sister kept lobbing questions like she was interviewing the two of them for an entertainment news magazine.

"So, what was it about Katie that convinced you to be exclusive, Ben? I wanna hear more about that spark."

Katie turned to Ben with a lifted brow, anxious to see how he would handle this one. "Yes, Ben. Do tell us more about that spark."

"The spark?" Ben's grin was wide as he ran his hand along the back of his neck and then rubbed it over the top of his head. "How do you explain a spark? There isn't much to tell. It's either there or it isn't. And with Kate, it's there. Without a doubt." He looked at Katie then, their eyes locking. "I've never felt a connection like this before."

His voice on that last part was quieter, like a soft caress for her alone. His gaze dropped to her mouth and lingered there, and a phantom tingle danced across her lips with the memory of the kiss they'd shared. Somewhere deep inside her, a warmth began to spread, melting her from the inside out.

Warning alarms went off in her head, and she looked away to escape the spell she was under. Gulping down the remainder of her water, she ignored Ben's quiet chuckle on her left side and Laura's raving about how romantic his answer was on the right.

For far too long, Katie had been both lonely and alone, yearning for companionship, connection, and love, even before the shell of a relationship she had with Grant ended.

To be the object of Ben's attention felt incredible, and she longed to lean into that feeling and bask in it. But she desperately needed to keep herself in check. She couldn't afford to forget that none of this was real, not even the tenderness in his touch as he reached to take her hand.

As the meal drew to a close and the family retreated to the restaurant lobby to say good night, everyone seemed to be in good spirits except Lydia, who had remained quiet through dessert.

Katie was exhausted, but she managed to keep a smile plastered on her face, even though she felt like she'd been put through an emotional wringer.

"Where do we go tomorrow?" Martin asked.

"Coconut Palms Cay, Daddy," Laura said, looping her arm through his. "Ben and Katie, we've rented a cabana for everyone, so the two of you can plan on joining us there if you'd like. It's supposed to have a waiter who'll come around and take our drink orders, but we'll still need to go to the pavilion for food."

"Sounds good," Ben said as he gave Brady a high five. "Katie and I booked a couple of activities, but I'm sure we'll stop by at some point."

"Great. We plan on being there all day, or as long as Brady wants to stay."

"I will not be out in the heat all day," Lydia announced.

"That's okay, Mom," Laura said. "You can come and go whenever you want. Oh, Ben, it's Bungalow Four."

"Got it. See you guys tomorrow."

He and Katie walked away, and once they were out of earshot, he said, "I think that went well; how about you? I mean, everyone survived. No one threw food or flipped a table. I'll count that as a success."

"Please don't bring up my writing again."

"I won't. I didn't know it was a sensitive subject, or I never would have mentioned it, I swear. Maya's told me that she thinks you're incredibly talented, and that you've always wanted to publish a novel but you've been too busy working on other people's books. She sounded excited that you were going to focus on your own stuff now that you have more time, so I thought you'd be excited too. I could tell after the fact that wasn't the case, so I did what I could to put the cat back in the bag, so to speak. I shouldn't have assumed. I should have asked you first, and I'm sorry. I really did tell them because I think it's cool that you're a writer."

"It's okay. It's just that I...you're right. It's a sensitive subject."

They continued in silence for a bit, and then Ben said, "I'm not sure where we're headed, but there are plenty of options depending on what you'd like to do. There's a musical in the main theater starting soon. The piano bar should be open as well as the other lounges. Or we could go up on the top deck and check out the view. It's supposed to be a clear night."

"Can I get a raincheck? I don't know if it was getting up so early this morning to catch the plane or if it's just all the tension of the day, but I'm tired. I need sleep. Obviously, you can go and do whatever you'd like. I don't want to keep you from having fun."

"Are you kidding me?" Ben laughed. "It's taking all I have to stay awake right now. My body is still struggling to figure out what time zone it's in, and all that sugar in the dessert didn't exactly help."

"Why did you suggest a musical or a piano bar if all you want is sleep?"

"I dunno." Ben shrugged with a sheepish grin. "It's your first cruise, and I didn't want it to be lame."

"Lame? Please." She swept her hand toward the main atrium as they entered it. "Look at this place. This is not lame. My life in New York two months ago? That was lame. This? This is amazing. So, I'm good. Please do not do anything on this trip that you don't want to do just because you think I want to. Promise?"

"I don't know if I can make that promise. I feel like I'm kind of in the host role here, so I'm responsible for making sure you have a good time. I promised Maya—"

"I don't care what you promised Maya. You aren't responsible for me, Ben. Tell me you understand that."

"I do...well, on some level I do, but we did come on this cruise together, and part of traveling with another person is being willing to do some things they want to do."

"True, okay, well, I might be up for something more entertaining tomorrow night after I've gotten some rest, but tonight, what I want to do is go back to the room, brush my teeth and take off my makeup, and then put on my pajamas and go to bed."

"Then that's what we'll do. The elevators are this way."

ELEVEN

I n all the chaos of dinner, Katie completely forgot about
the issue with the sleeping arrangements, but she was
relieved to find that someone had addressed it when they
returned to the room.

The sofa cushions had been removed, and a twin size
sleeper had been pulled from its base and dressed in sheets
and a blanket. A curtain had been pulled shut between the
sofa and the bed, dividing the room into two parts and
allowing both sleep spaces to have privacy.

"I'll take the sofa," Ben said. "You can have the bed."

"No way. You're way too big for a twin, and I think
that's even smaller than a standard twin. I'll take the sofa,
and you take the bed."

"I can't do that." His nose wrinkled in distaste. "I try to
have a modern mindset, and I'm all for equal rights and
equal pay. But in a situation like this, I must be a gentleman
and give up the bed. I wouldn't feel right otherwise."

"Gentleman or not, I wouldn't feel right sleeping in
that huge bed while your feet and one whole side of your

body hang off the sofa. Don't be ridiculous. I sleep on a twin bed at Maya's, so I'll be fine. I'm taking the sofa."

"If you insist, milady," he said with a dramatic bow. "Thank you. I appreciate your consideration and your generosity. Now, would you like for me to leave the room so you can get changed for bed and do whatever you need to in private?"

"No, I can change in the bathroom with the door closed, and everything else I need to do takes place in there as well."

Once she'd finished with her toiletries, she offered to wait on the balcony while Ben got changed for bed with the drapes drawn.

It had been a warm day, but the night air rolling in off the water carried a chill with it that made her wish she'd thought to grab a sweatshirt.

The waves were calmer than she'd expected, and their gently rolling motion kept going as far as the eye could see, disappearing into the horizon so that she couldn't tell where the water ended, and the sky began.

Without the brilliant light of the sun reflecting off it, the water was black, devoid of any color unless she looked straight down to where the lights cast from the ship illuminated the top of the crests in a deep sapphire blue.

Looking down intrigued her, but it was also incredibly unsettling. She had no concept of how much distance was between her and the sandy bottom, but she knew it was a long way down. She shuddered at the thought of how many creatures could be swimming beneath her, unseen in those pitch-black depths.

The moon was on the other side of the ship, hidden from her view, but the sky was clear, and there were more stars than she'd ever seen in a single night.

"Beautiful, isn't it?" Ben said as he slid the door open and stepped out onto the balcony.

"Breathtaking."

"It's chilly, huh? You good? You need a jacket?"

"Yeah, I was gonna grab my sweatshirt once you were done."

"Here," he said, reaching inside the door to grab his hoodie. "Just put this on."

"Thanks."

She settled into one of the chairs, and he sat next to her, propping his feet on the railing. They sat in silence, each of them lost in their own thoughts as the sound of the waves and the view of the constant roll of the water soothed them.

Her mind was relentless, replaying every moment of the day and evening, obsessing over everything she felt she'd gotten wrong or wished she'd said differently.

She couldn't go back and change any of it, but there was one topic that she could at least offer further explanation on. He hadn't asked for it, but for reasons she didn't care to analyze too deeply, she cared what Ben thought and wanted him to understand.

"Hey, about the writing thing...I know I probably overreacted, but the thing is...writing has been part of my identity for practically my entire life. It's what I always wanted to do, what I felt like I was supposed to do. I've always been good at it, and it came easy for me. Whenever I imagined my future, success was being a writer. But now, I'm scared that maybe I'm actually not a writer, and that's why it's such a sensitive subject."

"What do you mean? Why would you suddenly not be

a writer? Is this because you're not published yet? That's not what makes you a writer."

She let out a heavy sigh as she zipped his hoodie higher and shoved her hands into the pockets.

"The truth is I haven't been able to write in...years. It's like my stories all dried up and went away. I sit down and stare at a blank page or a blank screen, and nothing will come. When I was younger, I always had characters talking in my head, all the time. Entire stories played out up there with dialogue and settings and plot twists galore. By the time I was in high school, I'd often be working on three or four stories all at one time with more on the back burner waiting for a turn."

Ben smiled. "I get that way with projects sometimes. Like they all want to be top priority and they're jockeying for position so they can be completed first."

"Exactly. But then, little by little, they all went quiet. I think it started in college, and by the time I got to New York, I realized it was a problem, but my job was so demanding, and I was so stressed all the time that I couldn't devote any headspace to worrying about that. I thought for a while that was the problem—that I simply didn't have any energy left to create. I also wondered if having a job I hated in publishing somehow tainted it for me, like a negative association thing. Once I realized that I couldn't write, even when I really wanted to, then I kind of panicked. I tried everything to force a story out, but the more I pushed..."

"The harder it became?"

She nodded as she stared out at the water. "So, I just stopped trying. I can't tell you the last time I wrote something. Not even a story. A poem. A letter. Anything. No one else knows." She glanced over at him and back at the water. "I don't even know why I'm telling you, other than I felt like If I didn't tell someone, I was going to go mad. It's like this dark secret I'm hiding, and I don't want anyone to know. My sister always asks if I've written anything, and I've been telling her I was just too busy. So, of course, since I got laid off, now she thinks that I'll be doing so much writing. She even bought this chair at the thrift store to put in my room because she said it called to her and told her it was a writing chair."

Ben smiled with a subtle nod, like he understood completely how something like that could happen with Maya.

"She has no clue," Katie said, her voice breaking as her eyes filled with tears. "No one does. No one knows how bad it is—that I can't write at all. So, now that I got laid off, everyone expects me to finally get around to finishing something, and God, I wish I could, but it's just not there. It's gone." She wiped the back of her hand across her eyes. "My talent is gone, and now, they're all gonna know, and I'm gonna let them all down."

"You're not letting anyone down, Kate," Ben said, his voice calm and soothing as he pulled his feet from the railing and turned so that he faced her.

"I'm so scared." Her tears began to come faster, and she put her hands over her eyes to hide them. "What if it never comes back? What if I can't write again? If this is all I ever wanted to be, and I can't be this, then who am I?"

He scooted his chair closer and reached to stroke his hand up and down her back, and while the strength emanating from his presence was comforting, it also made her cry harder.

"Shh, c'mon. It's okay." Cradling his arm around her shoulders, he pulled her toward his chest and held her as best as he could with them seated in separate chairs.

Her emotions had taken her beyond worrying about what he thought or whether it was appropriate to seek such solace from a stranger. She buried her face in his chest and sobbed, releasing some of the energy that had held her so tightly strung.

Once the initial wave of overwhelm had passed, she sat up, rubbing her knuckles beneath her nose. "I'm sorry," she whispered, but Ben shook his head and shushed her, his arm still around her shoulders.

"You don't have to apologize. You needed to let it out."

"Maybe so," she said with a throaty cry chuckle, "but I didn't have to let it out all over you."

"It's all right. This T-shirt's cotton. It'll dry. Besides, what's a little more saltwater when you're sitting outside breathing in sea air? Stay here. I'll be right back."

He returned with a box of tissues, which she took with a grateful laugh. "Thanks."

After giving her a moment to compose herself, he said, "I understand what you're going through. I've been in a similar situation, and it's scary, frustrating, and unsettling when you can't access what's always been a part of you. When you feel like you can't be who you truly are or do the things you were born to do. Some people create better under pressure, but for me...and I suspect for you as well... that pressure stifles us and shuts us down. So, you may be right about the stress and the negative association from work. Add to that exhaustion, heartache, and not meeting other people's expectations, and it's the perfect storm for blocking."

"But that job's finished. It's done. Working at the surf shop, living with Maya, it's like a whole different world. Things are calm now, but I still don't have any voices in my head. Well, not the kind I want to hear anyway."

"It's only been like a month, Kate. You probably need more time to decompress. It takes the body a while to recover from the trauma of constant stress, not to mention the emotional toll. You lost your job, you made a big move, and it's never easy going through a break-up. Maya didn't give me any details, but she said it wasn't your decision. That it wasn't your choice."

"He found someone else."

"Ah." Ben nodded. "That sucks. Betrayal is a bitch to get over. I'm sorry."

"That's the easy answer, isn't it? *He found someone else.* You say that, and everyone's like, *okay, that's why it ended. That makes sense.* And they say they're sorry and move on. But our relationship didn't end because Grant found someone else. It's more like Grant found someone else because our relationship never should have been." She shifted to tuck her legs beneath her in the chair. "We really had nothing in common. And I mean, *nothing.* I hadn't dated anyone for a long time, and I'll admit... I wanted to be in a relationship. I wanted to have someone to go do things with. You know, watch a movie. Go to a concert. Take a walk in the park. Even just sit on opposite ends of the couch and read separate books at the same time. When I met Grant, he seemed so...*worldly.* He wasn't like anyone else I'd met. He was so knowledgeable about, like, everything. He'd been all over the world to all these places I'd only read about or seen in the movies. I thought he was cultured and sophisticated, but it was really more like he was snob. He had a magnificent loft apartment in a ritzy building in this awesome neighborhood, and he had connections all over town, so we always got ushered in the back door or seated in the VIP section."

"Was he older?" Ben asked.

"Yeah. Like ten years older, which at the time, I thought was cool. I thought all of it was cool when it started. Like this was the kind of person someone who lived in New York would date. This was the kind of guy a successful writer would date. That was the kind of apartment I'd always dreamed of when I thought about living in the city. That's what sad, really. I don't even miss Grant. We broke up not even a month ago, and he rarely even crosses my mind other than when I question why I was in it for so long. The thing I miss most was the apartment. God, I miss that apartment."

Ben chuckled, shifting his feet to the railing again. "That must have been a great apartment. How long were you with this guy?"

"Well, technically, almost two years. But we'd only been seeing each for four months when he got the transfer to London. We hadn't even had any conversations about being exclusive or what the future might hold. But because he was leaving, I felt like I was about to lose something and I needed to hold onto it, you know? Then when he mentioned that he might sublet his apartment while he was gone, we started talking about me moving in, and one thing led to another."

"You dated for almost two years, and he was gone over a year of that?"

"He was gone fifteen months, yeah. I sound pretty dumb right now, don't I?"

"No, that's not what I was thinking at all."

"What were you thinking?"

He turned his head to look at her, his face unreadable in the shadows of darkness. "I was thinking that when you came to Florida for that concert, he'd just left for London. So, you'd only been dating four months, and you hadn't made a serious commitment yet, other than subletting the guy's apartment. Hmm."

"What?"

"I should have tried a lot harder." He stood before she could process his words and question what he meant. Stretching his arms over his head with a big yawn, he went to the door and then turned back to her. "When I feel myself going into burnout or reaching a shutdown, I try to step away completely for a bit. I don't pick up a brush or a tool. I don't even step inside the studio. Instead, I try to fill my creative well with things that bring me joy. I spend time with nature. I visit a place I've never been. I read a book from an author I've never read. It sounds like your well ran dry, and you can't pull from an empty well. I think you need to give yourself some grace and spend some time focusing on joy. When you're in a good place, you'll find your muse again. For now, set it aside and let it go."

"I just told you I haven't written anything in years, so I think it's been set aside for a while already."

"You may have set it aside physically, but you haven't done it emotionally. Not in here." He bumped his fist to his chest. "Let go. Find your joy. Find your peace. You'll never stop being a writer, Kate. It's who you are. You just need to get quiet enough in your own head that you can hear the voices again. I gotta get some sleep. Feel free to leave the door open if you want so you can hear the ocean. It should be chilly enough that it won't get stuffy without the AC." He smiled, and even though it was muted by the darkness, it was enough to make her melt.

"Thanks. For...you know."

"G'night, Kate. Remember the mantra: Tomorrow is going to be a great day. You're going to have the time of your life. Now you just need to believe it."

Twelve

Katie had been so tired at the end of dinner that she was certain she'd be asleep the moment her head hit the pillow. But it had been three hours since she'd laid down on the little sofa bed, and she was still wide awake.

She'd stayed out on the balcony for almost an hour after Ben went in, replaying their conversation in her head.

What had he meant by saying he should have tried harder? Had he been interested in her the night they met? Was there more truth to his story about the spark than she'd realized?

But that made no sense. If he'd been hitting on her that night, she was certain she'd remember. Grant or no Grant, if a guy like Ben was paying her attention, she'd notice. Wouldn't she?

Then again, if he'd been that into her, why hadn't he told Maya? She was certain her sister would have told her, but Maya had only ever mentioned Ben in regard to their friendship, nothing more.

He'd said try *harder*. How hard did he really try? And did he ever intend to try again?

What would her response be if he did?

She couldn't deny there was an attraction there. She'd become hyper aware of every time he brushed against her in the elevator or the hall, and she'd taken to inhaling more deeply when he was close by just get a whiff of his cologne.

She'd suspected it might be mutual. There were times she'd look up and catch him watching her, and he'd always unleash that easy smile, the one that never ceased to make her feel like an inferno inside. But he hadn't made any moves, and other than that weird comment on the balcony, he hadn't expressed any interest.

Plus, there was the little matter of them agreeing to fake a romance. It was to his advantage to play the role well to convince his family. How dumb would she be to fall for him and buy into their fairy tale for real?

With her brain tired and her body chilled, she'd gone back inside, tiptoeing past the bed to reach her side of the room.

But the sofa bed offered her no peaceful haven of slumber. It must have been made with a child in mind. Her toes bumped the end of the sofa with the slightest flexing of her foot, and though the end above her head wasn't touching her, having the barrier above and below her and the sofa back along her side made her feel like she was wedged in.

The thin mattress offered little comfort or support, and there was some type of metal frame running beneath it that hit right along her spine.

On top of that, the narrow bed creaked and groaned with any movement, so she couldn't even toss and turn. And the harder she tried to lie still and quiet, the more her body demanded that she move.

The bed was only part of the problem, though. Despite

her exhaustion, her mind refused to shut up and let her sleep.

She'd already re-analyzed every aspect of her move to New York, her relationship and break-up with Grant, her time with her sister, and a myriad of job possibilities for her future.

In an attempt to take Ben's advice to heart, she'd brainstormed a list of things she could do that might bring her joy and fill her well.

She'd counted down from a hundred twice, and when all else failed, she'd opened the reading app on her phone, figuring if she wasn't going to sleep, she might as get a few chapters in. But no story could hold her interest beyond the first couple of pages.

And she knew exactly why.

It was all because of the man lying on the other side of that curtain.

A man who seemed to know her even though she didn't know him.

She'd wondered before they embarked what it would be like to lie in bed knowing a stranger was lying in bed in the very same room. She'd worried that she might feel uncomfortable, vulnerable, or exposed.

In one way or another she'd already felt all those things on the very first night, but in none of the ways she'd imagined.

She still couldn't believe she'd sobbed all over Ben's chest, and though he'd joked about her saltwater tears, chances were there was some snot involved as well.

But God, it had felt so good to have his arms around her. To feel safe. Heard. Understood.

Ben let out a quiet moan and shifted in his sleep, reminding her of his presence in the room.

Not that her body ever forgot he was there. Her hormones seemed to be firing on all cylinders at the thought of the tall, dark, and handsome man lying all alone in a huge bed less than two feet away from her.

This trip had to be one of the craziest things she'd ever done.

Why did she think she could stay in a tiny room alone with this man for a week after months spent living alone and not be affected by his proximity?

I mean, granted, that should be possible. It shouldn't be an issue at all. It's not like she was an animal, unable to control her base instincts.

Tossing aside the blanket, she stood, thinking maybe she'd go back to the balcony and let the night air cool her skin again. While the temperature was fine without the AC, she needed the air to be moving.

She paused at the curtain. She'd come through his space earlier returning from the balcony, but to enter it again seemed like an invasion of his privacy. What if he woke and saw her standing there like Edward Cullen watching him sleep? Worse yet, what if she truly lost her mind and climbed into bed beside him?

Allowing her thoughts to continue to wander down that ridiculous path provided a pleasant mental journey, but it did nothing to cool her down. All it did was convince her that she needed to leave the room before she did something really stupid.

So, she shimmied out of her pajamas and into a pair of shorts and a T-shirt she'd pulled from the dresser in the dark. But when she tried to open the closet door to grab her sweatshirt, its hinge let out a piercing whine, so she froze, waiting and listening.

Ben changed his position in the bed, but he didn't give

any other indication he was awake, so she eased the closet door closed and grabbed his hoodie from the back of the chair instead.

The Lido deck was deserted in the wee hours, save for one small group of revelers who seemed determined to prolong the night as much as possible.

Katie made her way up to the top deck where she and Ben had watched the ship leave the port and head into the open waters.

Going to the rail, she looked down again, shuddering once more at the height and how black the water seemed. It was much darker from up here than it had been from their balcony, so far removed from the lights at the water's level that they cast no glow at all.

A chill ran up her spine at the thought of how terrifying it would be to fall overboard, and despite her aversion to the thought, she pictured herself plunging into that inky depth and being swallowed up by the night, never to be seen again.

Backing away from the rail with another shudder, she looked around for a lounge chair, disappointed to see that they'd all been stacked and put away. Wandering toward the rear of the ship where they'd seen the more secluded pool earlier, she was thrilled to see that the large, round wicker chairs were still out, even though their cushions had been packed away for the night.

She started to climb inside one, but the large half dome covering it would hinder her ability to see anyone approaching, and though she felt safe alone on the deck, she knew it would be irresponsible to put herself in such a vulnerable position with no way out.

Standing at the rail at the rear of the ship, she looked down at the frothy water churned by the massive engines. A pale trail of foam snaked into the darkness behind them, and her mind turned macabre again as she imagined what it would be like to fall overboard and watch the ship move away, the glittering lights growing smaller until it disappeared and left you in utter and total darkness.

With a shiver and a shake to dispel the image, she took a step back and turned her focus up to the night sky. She'd found the view beautiful from their balcony, but here, atop the ship and unencumbered by anything surrounding her, she was blown away by the enormity of the sky. Never had she seen it look so huge, like a gigantic dome covering the earth, yet it wasn't a dome at all. It was open and endless, stretching on far beyond what any human eye could ever see. The longer she focused on any one spot, she'd see another star appear, and then another behind it, and another beyond that. They were infinite, and she'd never felt so small and insignificant on the planet.

Even the enormous ship with all its thousands of people and numerous decks stacked on top of one another was nothing but a dot in a vast body of water on the surface of a planet that was only one of many in a galaxy among an unknown number of galaxies.

Emotion welled within her as she let go of everything else and just acknowledged the wonder in that moment.

She smiled, knowing Maya would be proud of her for committing to be in the present so fully. Her sister was right when she'd said this was like being on another planet. It was overwhelming, but in trying to comprehend it, she'd taken her mind off her little and ultimately inconsequential problems.

A cold wind swept up from the water and blasted her, whipping her hair across her face and chilling her to the bone. Lifting the hood over her head, she hugged Ben's jacket more tightly around her. It carried his scent, and she turned her face into the hood, reaching up to press the fabric against her skin as she breathed him in.

Enveloped in the faint hint of his cologne, she couldn't help but recall the way it felt to be held in his embrace on the balcony. She imagined what it would be like if he was here now, not as Ben the semi-stranger who was pretending to be in love with her, but as someone she knew and respected. Someone she'd traveled with often. Someone who made her feel safe and seen despite the incomprehensible magnitude of existence beyond theirs. Someone who truly loved her for who she was and would be willing to make their love a priority.

And while she was at it, she wanted someone passionate, affectionate, and loving. Someone who wanted to hold hands when they walked down the sidewalk or who'd rest his hand on her thigh in a movie. Someone who'd brushed her hair off her face and tucked it behind her ear. Someone who'd kiss her forehead.

She wanted to feel dizzy after every kiss, the same way she'd felt when Ben had kissed her. Or when she'd kissed Ben. She still wasn't sure who was kissing who by the end.

Pretend or not, he'd certainly been all in for that kiss, and she had too. In fact, thinking back on it, she was certain the attraction between them had to be mutual on some level. That kind of instantaneous chemistry would be hard to fake, and she wondered how that moment might have progressed if they hadn't had his mother for an audience.

It wasn't likely to happen again, unfortunately. She couldn't conceive of any occasion where they'd be with his family and need to spontaneously share another kiss, and it wasn't like affection in front of your parents, siblings, and nephew was something you planned for. Especially not with a family who seemed as emotionally distant as his.

"There you are!" Ben said from across the deck behind her, and she spun with a little scream.

THIRTEEN

"Geez, you scared the crap outta me."

So much for being alert and aware of her surroundings!

"Sorry. That wasn't my intent. Quite the opposite, actually. I was calling out to make sure you knew I was here before I got closer. What are you doing up here all by yourself?"

"I couldn't sleep, and after a few hours of lying there staring at the ceiling, I figured I'd stare at the stars instead."

He looked up at the sky and grinned. "Plenty of them out tonight, for sure. Did you see the moon?" He pointed his thumb over his shoulder toward the front of the ship on the other side.

She turned in that direction and couldn't believe she hadn't noticed the moon as she was geeking out over the sky. It was almost full and likely would be before the end of their cruise.

"You've got to be kidding me. How did I not see that? I guess I never looked in that direction." She walked over to the rail to get a better look and then she gasped at the reflection of the moon dancing across the waves. "Look! Wow. That's beautiful."

Ben nodded, his hands in his pockets and his arms held tight against his ribs. "Yeah. When the moon's full, I love to go over to the beach and watch it rise. To see how the colors shift and fade and bleed into each other as the sun disappears behind you and the moon rises to take its place. I never get tired of seeing the moonlight on the water."

He shivered a bit, and she realized she was wearing his jacket.

"Oh, my gosh. I have your coat. I'm so sorry. I tried to open the closet, but it was loud, and I didn't want to wake you. I planned to be back before you needed it."

She started unzipping it to take it off, but he motioned for her to stop.

"It's okay, keep it on. I don't need it. I'm wearing jeans. You're the one in shorts, so you're probably colder than me."

"Yeah, well, the shorts were the first thing I found in the dark."

"Makes sense. I take it the bed wasn't very comfortable, huh?"

"No, it's fine." She waved her hand in dismissal. "I just have so much on my mind. I couldn't seem to shut everything down and sleep. Did I wake you when I left? Why are you up?"

Shrugging, he said, "I have no idea what woke me. It could just be that my body still thinks it's in Barcelona. Six hours ahead, so I'd already be at the gallery and on my 2nd cup of coffee by now. But instead, I stumbled out of bed and eased the curtain open to go to the bathroom, and it was only on my way back to bed that I realized you weren't even there. Startled me, to be honest. Figured I should come look for you."

"Sorry. I should have left a note or something. I've been meaning to ask you what you're doing in Barcelona. Maya said you've been there for a month? I take it you're working at a gallery there?"

"Yes. I was selected for a residency program in conjunction with a small museum that houses an art gallery and studio on its grounds." He leaned his hip against the railing as he talked." They offer me free room and board and art supplies, and in return, I help out in the gallery and give occasional tours of the museum. And of course, I spend a lot of time touring around the area, finding inspiration."

"That sounds amazing. How long will you be there?"

"Probably three more months, if I don't decide to extend. It's a beautiful city, and the people at the gallery are lovely. So, I may stay, I don't know yet."

"Do you travel around a lot then?"

"Yeah, I'd say I've done my fair share the last few years. It's starting to wear on me a bit. I don't think I'd ever give it up completely, but I am starting to miss my own bed and my own studio. I may shove my passport in a drawer and stay home for a while. At least until I get the itch to go again."

"Where's home?"

"Oh, Cocoa Beach. I have a house there, not too far from Maya's. If you don't mind my saying, you seem to be shivering an awful lot. Do you want to go back inside?"

"Yes but no. I don't know. I am cold, but I don't want to go back in yet. It's just so surreal being up here, just the two of us with the sky, the moon, and the stars. It's very other-worldly."

"It is. Might I suggest that we retreat to that lounger

over there? The dome lid might at least help to block the wind."

"Yeah, I started to sit there before, but I was worried about someone coming up behind me and me not hearing them." She rolled her eyes. "Clearly, I should have been a little more diligent about that."

"We could probably turn it and have it face this way. That way we could see anyone who comes back here, and we could also see the moon."

"Great idea!"

Once they'd gotten the lounger situated where they wanted it, they crawled inside it, and then Ben looked at her with his hands outstretched. "I don't wanna be presumptuous or anything, but would you like to huddle together? You know, sit close to combine our body heat and shut out the cold? I swear I'll be honorable."

"Well, considering that I'm wearing your jacket, I guess the least I could do is sit close enough to share it with you."

She took the jacket off as he sat back against dome, and then he lifted his arm for her to sit next to him. She nestled into him as he spread the jacket over them, and then she pulled her knees to her chest so her legs could be covered as well.

The moon was directly in front of them, giving them their own personal planetarium show.

"I've always wanted to travel," she said once they were settled in and starting to feel warmer.

"Then, I'm sure you will someday."

"I don't know. Kind of hard to travel without a job or a paycheck."

"Unless you find a job that allows you to travel and work at the same time. Which is what I did."

"I don't know what I'm doing next. My whole life, I've

had a grand plan. And now? I have no idea what I'm doing."

"Do you know what you want to do?"

"I want to write, but for reasons we've already discussed and other economic ones, that's not a viable possibility. Not right now, anyway." She leaned her head back to look up at him. "Did you really quit law school to become an artist? If you don't mind my asking."

"I don't. But no, I didn't give up law to *become* an artist. That's already who I was. I just decided to stop being who I wasn't."

She laid her head against his chest as she considered that. It sounded like a noble concept, but she would have to figure out who she was before she could determine who she wasn't.

"Is that what made your mom angry with you?" she asked, wary of broaching the subject, but eager to know why Lydia was so nasty to Ben. She'd heard her mention something about addicts when she was coming out of the bathroom. She'd gotten the idea it was regarding Ben dating someone Lydia didn't approve of, but Ben had said it happened when he was nineteen. Twelve years was a long time to be angry about your son's ex-girlfriend.

"My mom is angry with me for many reasons, and I've had to accept that there isn't really anything I can do about any of them. There's not anything I'm willing to do, anyway. But you can believe me when I say I tried."

"I do." She wanted to know more, but it seemed like a sensitive subject, so she'd do for him what he'd done for her and leave it alone. So instead, she broached another possibly sensitive subject she was curious about. "How much of what you told your family about the night we met was true? Did you really sit at my table on purpose?"

"Yes, I did. I sat next to you, in fact."

"What? No way."

"Way. I shared my nachos with you. You kept flicking the olives over to my side."

She sat up, knocking the jacket from them as she twisted to face him. "That was you? Oh my god. No way. But you had, like, a massive beard. It was braided, right? And your hair was long and tangly, and you had some kind of thing wrapped around your head."

"Yeah," he said, chuckling. "I'd just gotten back from spending three months in the Alaskan wilderness, and I was still holding onto a bit of that. Not quite ready to let the experience go, I guess. I went in for a shave and a haircut not long after that night, but you were already back in New York by then."

"I can't believe that was you. I couldn't understand why I didn't remember you, but now that I know you looked completely different, it makes a little more sense. Did we talk a lot? Did we have any meaningful conversations?"

Ben shook his head, laughing. "No. To be honest, I was a little shell-shocked that night. It was the first time I'd been around that many people in a while. And I also think I was a little bit in awe of you. Feeling kind of shy and fully realizing I wasn't presenting as my most attractive self. So, I hung back and let the other guys talk, but I listened to everything you had to say. And I shared my nachos. Not that I had a choice. They got delivered and you just started eating them. I think you thought they were for the table, so I didn't correct you. And I didn't mind. It gave me a reason to interact with you between Paul being a pompous jerk and Michael being all smarmy."

"Ah, yes, I do remember Michael. And yes, smarmy is the perfect word for him. But I feel bad that I mooched your nachos. I'm sorry. Can I make it up to you somehow? Do they serve nachos anywhere on the ship?"

He smiled, shaking his head as he rubbed his hand over the back of his neck. "I don't know. It's fine. I'm having a conversation with you all alone with no other guys around, so I'd say this is payback enough."

Their gazes locked, and that heat blossomed inside her again. He must feel it. He had to. He was telling her he was interested, wasn't he? But he wasn't making any move to kiss her, even though they were all alone and snuggled into a secluded chair with their faces only inches apart.

Thinking of the kiss took her back to the one they'd shared.

"Were you shocked when I kissed you?"

"Shocked? Yeah. Of course. It came out of nowhere. But I'm not one to refuse a gift, you know?"

"Do you think your mom bought it? Like, do you think your family believes that we're head over heels in love?"

"I don't know. Obviously, I haven't been alone with any of them to hear what they think."

"We really should have planned out a backstory. We should have come up with the most fabulous first meeting and first date. Something incredibly romantic."

"More romantic than nachos and debates about bodice rippers?"

She laughed as she settled back in against his chest, pulling the jacket up over them again.

"Who would we be? How did we meet?"

His shoulder shrugged beneath her head. "I don't know. You're the writer."

"Don't say that. You know I can't write right now. So, help a girl out. How'd we meet? *Pretend* us, not *real* us."

"Maybe I got into your car, thinking it was an Uber," Ben said.

"Ugh. It's already been done. Maybe we both had golden retrievers and we met at a dog park."

"Do they shed? I have allergies."

She leaned back and looked up at him again. "Just because *you* have allergies doesn't mean Pretend Ben has allergies. Pretend Ben can be any way you want him to be. That's the beauty of fiction."

"Okay well, I think it's best if we keep the pretend version as close to the real ones as possible. What if we're pretending and someone brings a dog, and then I start sneezing? It would blow our cover." He paused and then looked down at her. "Wait...I'm confused. Are we going to pretend to be these versions of ourselves? Or are we just coming up with a backstory for fun?"

"Fun. If it doesn't have to be believable, it can be much more interesting."

Adjusting his legs and shifting his back against the seat, he hugged her closer to him. "Okay. Let's see. I think I want to be a spy."

"It's a cruise ship. What would you be spying on?"

"You said it doesn't have to be believable."

"True. Okay. You're a spy, and I'm an assassin. We're both targeting the same international arms dealer, and he happens to be on this cruise. Being the diligent and observant people we are, we noticed that we were both following him, and we confronted each other and fell in love."

"Just like that?"

"Just like that."

"Okay," he said.

They sat there snuggled together for a few more

minutes in silence, enjoying the solitude, the warmth, and the closeness.

Then Katie said. "I don't know that I'm really cut out to be an assassin. All the killing and the blood. Maybe we should be something more low-key. More ordinary. But still romantic."

"Maybe we're on our honeymoon. We just got married on the beach in Cocoa, and we drove to Miami the morning after the wedding and set sail."

"Hmm...too ordinary. How about this? We were high school sweethearts who went to separate out of state colleges, and our lives grew apart. But then we ended up sitting next to each other in the same row on the same airplane, and we discover that we both live in the same city now."

"I feel like something like that has been done before."

"Yeah, you're probably right. Is it just me, or is it getting colder?" She yawned and wriggled even closer.

Wrapping his other arm around her, he tucked his chin over her head. "It is a little colder. You ready to head back inside? At some point, you need to get some sleep."

"Yeah, but I want to figure this out first. Maybe you were painting in a courtyard at a small boutique hotel in Italy. I'd gone there to write, and it was my first day in the village. I stopped you and asked for directions, and my Italian was horrible, so we laughed when we discovered we were both American. We ended up going to dinner together and sharing a pasta dish—I asked this time if it was okay that we share. We were both there for the next month, so we spent every moment together. And at the end of the month, I'd written you into my book as the hero, and you'd painted me into your courtyard."

"Did I propose in the courtyard?" Ben whispered.

"No. It was too soon, and because we'd met each other while we were traveling and living under idyllic circumstances, we decided it was impossible to know if it would work in the context of our real lives."

"But we're still together. We're on a cruise. So, we made it work? Right?"

"Yeah, of course. It's not a romance without a happy ending."

"Whew," Ben exhaled. "I feel better knowing we were able to make it work. Love should always conquer all."

He moved to stand, and then he offered her his hand to pull her up with him. "C'mon. Let's get you back inside before you turn into a popsicle."

Katie felt a pang of disappointment. She'd gotten so wrapped up in the story that she'd been expecting a kiss, but the story was Pretend Ben and Pretend Katie. And it wasn't real life.

FOURTEEN

"You're taking the bed," Ben said when they came back into the room.

"No. There is no way you would get a single minute of sleep on that sofa, Ben."

"And obviously, neither will you. You take the bed and I'll pull the pillow and blanket off the sofa and sleep on the floor."

"What? No way. Look, there must be a better way to do this. We're both adults, right? We're capable of keeping our hands and other body parts to ourselves, aren't we?" She said a silent prayer hoping she'd be able to. "Let's just share the bed. It's plenty big enough for both of us to have our own side. We can even create a pillow barrier down the middle so there's no question where one side ends or another begins. Here, look."

She grabbed the extra pillow from the sofa along with the throw pillow the steward had set aside, and then she stripped back the sheet and blanket from the bed. After arranging the extra pillows in a line down the middle, she stood at the foot of the bed to ensure it was relatively even, and then she pulled the covers up over them.

"Do you mind if I take the side by the balcony so I can hear the water?"

"Not at all," Ben said, "but are you sure you won't be too cold?"

"I'll pull the blanket from the sofa and put it over me just in case. It'll be fine."

She hoped it would be fine, but she wasn't at all sure. It had been impossible to sleep with him on the bed and her on the couch; how on earth would she be able to lay there knowing he was within arm's reach yet out of reach?

At the same time, there was no way she'd rest if he was on the floor or the tiny sofa bed because of her.

This was the only reasonable solution. Her only hope was that she'd finally reached a level of exhaustion that would let her just pass out and be oblivious to Ben lying next to her.

"Katie?"

She heard the voice from far off in a distant land. It was deep but soft. Vaguely familiar but she couldn't place it.

"Katie?"

It came again, a little louder this time, and while something inside her felt happy to hear it, she also wanted to turn away from it and stay in the cocoon of warmth she was wrapped in. But then the soft ground on which she lay began to shift beneath her, and she sat up with a start, suddenly wide awake.

"Sorry," Ben said softly. "My arm was asleep, and when

I tried to move it out from under you, you grabbed onto it and wouldn't let go."

"Oh my God." She rubbed her hands over her face and squinted against the sunlight streaming through the open door. "What time is it?"

"It's ten."

"I slept until ten? I haven't done that since...I don't think I've ever slept until ten."

"Well, it was almost four by the time we went to bed."

The reminder that they'd gone to bed together jarred her from her sleep fog, and she looked down to find the pillow barrier askew and her lying entirely on Ben's side of it.

"I'm sorry," she said, rushing to scoot back to her side.

"Don't be. I think you must have gotten cold in your sleep and were just seeking out warmth. It's a survival tactic."

"Right. Because I wouldn't have survived the freezing temperatures of a Caribbean cruise ship if I hadn't found you in the night. Thank God you were here." She rubbed her palm against her forehead and then took the elastic band from her hair. "I really am sorry. I hope I didn't do or say anything inappropriate in my sleep, and I hope you were able to get some rest, despite my needing warmth."

"You were fine. Nothing inappropriate, and I didn't mind keeping you warm. Well, not until my arm went to sleep anyway."

"Wait...did you say I was lying *on* your arm? Like, long enough for it to go to sleep?"

"Yeah. It's okay. There were a few pins and needles when you sat up, but the blood flow's all good now."

"Why didn't you wake me up before?"

"Because I figured you needed the sleep. And like I said,

I didn't mind. To be honest, it was nice lying there with you as the sun came up and the light starting streaming across the room. I liked it. It seemed like a moment Cruise Ben and Cruise Katie would have shared."

"Cruise Ben and Cruise Katie? That sounds like a special edition Barbie couple. They probably come with their own life preservers or something. Color coordinated to their outfits, of course."

"Isn't that what you called the pretend versions of us last night?"

Tossing back the covers, she climbed out of bed and headed for the bathroom. "I called them Pretend Ben and Pretend Katie, but I think Cruise Ben sounds like a more interesting guy. Let's go with that."

She closed the bathroom door, but then as his words registered, she opened it and stepped out to stare at him. "Did you say you watched the sun coming up? How long have you been awake, and how long have I been stopping the blood flow in your arm?"

"I've been dozing off and on for a few hours. Still adjusting to the time change, I guess."

"Hours? I laid on your arm for hours? Why didn't you say something?"

"Maybe because I didn't want it to end?"

She didn't know what to say to that, so she just turned and went back into the bathroom.

"Hey, I was thinking in between dozes this morning," he said once she'd emerged from the bathroom with a freshly washed face and her teeth brushed. "And I know this is probably going to sound crazy, but considering that we now have three different versions of our lives going concurrently, maybe not."

"Three? How do we have three?"

He held up his fingers as he counted them off. "One, there's the truth. We met once. I didn't make nearly the impression you did, and we met again at the airport before boarding this cruise. Two," he lifted the second finger, "Same story as the first, but with the added chapters being you volunteered to pretend to be my love interest in front of my family, and you blew my mind with one of the hottest kisses of my life, which happened to take place in front of my mother...and now that I say that out loud it sounds horrendous, and I definitely need more therapy."

"It does sound bad, but I'm more interested in that being one of the hottest kisses of your life. Really?"

"Yeah, why?"

She smiled as a warm flush crept into her cheeks. "Well, I mean, it was great and all, but it was a spur of the moment thing and I felt like I kind of came in hot. A little sloppy, even. I could do better. I'm sure of it. But I'm guessing the third would be Cruise Ben and Katie?"

He stared at her for a moment, his mouth slightly ajar and his fingers still holding the count in midair.

"What?" she asked.

"I don't even know. I'm still stuck on you thinking you could do better...okay, yeah, three is Cruise Ben and Katie, who have this fantastic Italian village backstory and they're solid, man. They've been through stuff, and they've had each other's backs, and they know where they stand. There's no games. There's no question. They don't have to dance around with everything they say and everything they do, worried they're gonna scare off the other person. They can just be themselves and know that's okay. If they wanna kiss, they kiss. If they wanna hold hands, they do it. And if Cruise Ben wants to lie there with Cruise Katie on his arm, watching the sun march across the room, and do it just because he loves the way she feels in his arms all snuggled against his side, then it's perfectly acceptable and not weird at all."

This time, Katie looked a little stunned and it took her a second to recover. "I never said it was weird or unacceptable. I just felt bad for putting your arm to sleep and forcing you to be immobile. For hours, evidently."

"I could have moved any time I wanted to. I didn't want to."

She blinked a couple of times as she weighed whether she wanted to ask him to expand on that, but then she opted to move on. "I'm sorry, but I got lost somewhere in all this. What was the point you were making about the three?"

He came and stood in front of her, reaching to take her hand in his. "In versions one and two, my family's nuts and my mother hates me. And I don't know what your story is in version two, but I know in the real life with no embellishments version, your life is a bit of a mess right now."

"Gee, thanks," she said, grinning.

"But in version three, we're golden. We're happy. Life is great, and this cruise is great, and it's everything we wanted it to be. We have the best possible outcome guaranteed, because we're making it up as we go along."

"Right, and that sounds awesome. Sign me up for that version, please! But we don't actually have that life, Ben. We made it up. We've got to live the one we've been given."

"Do we?" he asked, his eyes alight. "We're already pretending that we're dating anytime we're around my family, so we've suspended reality, have we not? Why can't we be Cruise Ben and Katie when it's just the two of us? When we get off this ship at the end of the week, we go back to our lives and our challenges and whatever the future brings. But for the next few days, let's be someone else. Someone who's happy with their life just the way it is."

She stared at him like he was bonkers, but she was also intrigued. Maya had said a cruise was an escape. Like unplugging from the real world for a few days.

She'd much rather be Cruise Katie with her picture-perfect life and her romantic hero boyfriend. If it was just between her and Ben and no one else knew, what would it matter? It wasn't like they were hurting anyone. And unlike the ruse they had going with his parents, they weren't lying to anyone other than themselves, and they both knew it was a lie.

"You're considering it, aren't you?" Ben grinned, giving her hand a light squeeze.

"This is insane. You do realize this is insane.

Ben nodded. "Yeah. But I still kinda wanna do it."

"I don't know. What would we do? Do we talk differently? Do we act differently? Do we have to constantly make up stuff? Because as we both know, my creativity is in the pits right now."

"We don't have to make up anything. You already did that when you created these characters. And as far as what we say or do, we just say or do whatever the character would. Just be the character,"

"But we can't actually be them." Katie moved past him to sit on the couch as she thought it through. "We'll still be ourselves. We'll still be those people we're running from."

"I know," he said, joining her on the couch. "That's why it's called pretend."

Katie rolled her eyes with a groan. "I get that, but children play pretend, Ben. We're adults."

"Adults play pretend all the time. It's called role play."

"Isn't that kind of like a bedroom thing, though?"

"Not necessarily. There are all sorts of games and activities that use role play. Think of this as a game where we have roles to play. And since this is our game that we're creating as we go, we make the rules of what it is and isn't. If we want to say sex is off the table, then there's no sex. I'd like to propose we have a rule that we can't lie to each other. That's the first rule. The cardinal rule. We can pretend as long as we're pretending together, but no lies between us."

"Okay, but we also need a rule that says either one of us can tap out whenever we want."

"Definitely," Ben nodded. "All we need to do is say *tapping out*. No lengthy explanation needed."

"I mean it. If it gets ridiculous or if we don't feel comfortable or it's not fun anymore, then either one of us can say *tapping out* and it ends. We go back to being us. Real life Ben and Katie. Deal?"

"Deal."

Katie was surprised at how natural it felt to slip into this role with Ben. She'd worried it would feel forced or require a conscious effort, but pretending to be his partner was no effort at all.

They walked hand in hand as they exited the ship and wandered down the meandering sidewalk of Coconut Palms Cay.

Ben's hand rested lightly on the small of her back as they waited in line to pick up their snorkeling equipment, and when they stopped to look in the shops along the beach, she found herself looping her arm through his without a second thought, as though they'd been touching for years.

It was a gorgeous day for outside activities, and the turquoise water was crystal clear, allowing Katie to see a multitude of brilliantly-colored fish and vibrant coral. They stayed in the water until their skin was like prunes, signaling each other whenever they found an interesting fish or a particularly beautiful coral.

"Did you have fun?" Ben asked when they returned the equipment.

"Yes," she said, gigging with delight. "I've never seen anything like that. This was amazing. Thank you!"

On impulse, she hugged him, not because it was something the pretend Katie would do, but because it was something *she* wanted to do.

Immediately, Ben's arms wrapped around her waist, and they stood there, holding each other without words as the water dripped from their skin onto the sand beneath them.

"I really enjoy your company," Ben said, pulling back just far enough for his eyes to search hers. "It just feels good to be around you. And the more time I spend with you, the more I want you in my life."

"Are we pretending right now? Is this Cruise Ben talking? Or Real Ben?"

Ben grinned, tightening his arms around her. "What do you say we head over to the dining pavilion and grab some lunch? Then maybe we'll see if we can find a couple of lounge chairs open and just kick back and relax for a while before we head back to the ship?"

She noticed he hadn't answered her question, but she

let it slide, not wanting to ruin the mood by pressing the matter. She knew Ben was interested in her. He'd said so several times, but not in those exact words. With the barrier of pretending to hide behind, he was much more open and free with his emotions and his affection. But that barrier prevented her from knowing what was real and what wasn't.

Not that she was complaining about the barrier. It benefitted her too. She certainly wasn't ready to pursue anything romantic yet. And even if she was, she couldn't see how this would work with Ben. When the cruise ended, he would go back to Barcelona, and she would return to Maya's to figure out her next steps. Having just ended a long-distance relationship, she had absolutely no desire to start another one. The next man she chose to be involved with needed to be local and capable of being fully present in her life.

The other complication she saw with Ben was that he was her sister's best friend. That was a powder keg destined to blow, and it could end badly for all involved.

So, no matter how much fun she was having with Ben or how strong the connection between them may be, she knew there was no future for them.

It was better for them to do it this way. To have their moment of pretend when they could be free to explore their attraction and their connection, untethered and uncomplicated. Then, when the cruise came to an end, so would they.

When they'd finished their lunch, Ben and Katie headed to the beach and found two empty lounge chairs. Pulling the chairs as close together as possible, they lay basking in the sun, laughing and talking in their own little world.

At some point, Katie drifted off to sleep, and when she woke, Ben was lying on his side with his arm flung across her waist, his face at peace in slumber.

She longed to trace her finger along his features, memorizing each and every one so she would have him in her heart when he was long gone from her side.

Something within her clenched at the thought, and she feared she'd already gone too far.

Would she be able to let go and say goodbye when the time came to stop pretending?

Closing her eyes again, she laid her arm over his, pulling him closer against her skin.

She refused to mourn the end before it came.

For today, she was Cruise Katie, and he was Cruise Ben, and she was safe in his embrace. After all, Cruise Katie already knew she'd be going home with Cruise Ben to their wonderful life together, so there was nothing for her to fear.

FIFTEEN

"I suppose we should stop by the cabana," Ben said once he and Katie returned the kayaks that afternoon. "Might as well go ahead and get it over with it."

She braced for his demeanor to change, which she had noticed seemed to happen when he had to interact with his family.

But to her surprise, his smile remained, and he remained cheerful and talkative as they walked toward the cabana holding hands.

She'd felt a bit of trepidation herself at the thought of another encounter with Lydia, but to her relief, Laura and Brady were the only ones present.

"Where is everyone?" Ben asked once he'd greeted his sister and been tackled by Brady.

"Oh, mom went back to the ship because she was getting too hot," Laura said from her lounge chair. "Dad and Dale felt like the server was taking too long to bring them drinks, so they both went to the bar. They said they'd be right back, but that was at least an hour ago."

Brady tugged on Ben's shorts. "Would you build a Sandcastle with me, Uncle Ben?"

"Of course, Braidster! We need to ask your mom first though."

Laura frowned as she adjusted the broad-rimmed straw hat on her head.

"I guess, but you have to stay where I can see you."

Brady jumped up and down, squealing in delight and then he took Ben's hand and began to pull him toward the water.

"Don't let him go anywhere near the water, Ben," Laura called out, and Ben turned back to look at her with a scowl.

"It's hard to build a sandcastle without wet sand, and in order to get wet sand, you have to go near the water."

"I don't want him in the water unless Dale or I are with him."

"Seriously? Do you not remember that I was a lifeguard for three summers."

Laura's lips protruded in a pout. "Yeah, well, that was like 15 years ago before you killed all your brain cells partying in college."

"Whatever," Ben said as turned to go. "It's not like I'm taking him out for a swim in the raging sea. We're just building a sandcastle."

"You have to watch him though."

"I realize that, Laura!'

His sister rolled her eyes but then smiled as she looked at Katie and patted the lounge chair next to hers. "Have a seat. I'm excited that we have a few minutes alone for some girl time. The server should be by soon and you can order whatever you'd like. They have a full bar."

"I'm not really much of a drinker."

"Oh. That's perfect for my brother."

Katie plopped down on the lounge chair and fixed her gaze on Ben and Brady, admiring the muscles in Ben's sculpted back as he dug a hole in the sand.

"Well, this is different," Laura said. "Nice, but different."

"What do you mean?"

"Ben hanging out with the family. Ben bringing a girl to meet the family. Ben laughing and smiling with someone other than Brady." She lowered her shades on the bridge of her nose and stared at Katie. "You're good for him. He seems happy."

Katie wasn't sure how to respond to that, so she just forced a smile and continued to watch the sandcastle construction.

"And don't worry about Mom," Laura said, adjusting her hat so she could lay her head back against the chair. "She's going to fight tooth and nail in the beginning, but I think eventually she'll get used to it."

Katie turned to her in confusion. "Get used to what?"

"You not being Allison." Laura sighed, crossing one ankle over the other. "She's always been convinced she could get them back together one day. She won't give that up easily, but hey, what can she do if he chooses you instead? Am I right?"

Katie knew the wise thing to do would be to politely nod and refuse to engage. Her romantic entanglement with Ben was strictly imaginary and would end when the cruise ended, so whether his mother preferred Allison was a moot point, and none of Katie's business or concern.

But she was concerned. Ben deserved to be happy, and

he had every right to choose whom to pursue that happiness with. As someone who had long struggled with her own domineering mother's inability to respect boundaries, Katie was outraged that Lydia would go to such lengths to try and control her son's love life. And the fact that everyone else in the family seemed to find it an acceptable status quo made her angrier.

"If he's not in love with Allison, why on earth would she want them together?"

Laura let out a derisive snicker. "For several reasons, and none of them have anything to do with love. Allison's family has been around forever. Old money, if you know what I mean. That's not just what they have in the bank account; it's also the power and connections that come with it. If my brother were to marry Allison, that would bolster my family's standing—and let's be honest...we're just talking about my mother here. None of the rest of us care."

"So, she wants him to marry someone he doesn't love so she can boost her social status?"

"You say that like it's nothing, but in the circles my mother travels in, it's everything. And it's not just about the exclusive lists my mother could get her name added to or the wealth Allison would bring to the marriage, though that certainly sweetens the deal. When Ben was with Allison, he stayed on the path. He was checking off all the boxes my mother had drawn for him. And when they broke up, he went way off path. And I mean way off."

Laura waved her hand through the air to illustrate her point, and then she took a sip of her drink before continuing.

"Ever since then, he's been like some kind of vagabond, living all over the world, never in the same place for more than a few months at a time, *never* coming home. And evidently, he's done with law, and he's convinced he's going to make it with the art thing. And I'm happy for him," she said in a tone that couldn't sound less genuine if she tried. "But it's like he's determined to do the absolute polar opposite of what Mom expected. I think she feels like Allison would be the key to reigning Ben back in. Allison kept him in line when they were together."

"Kept him in line?" Katie's indignation on his behalf swelled, and she found it hard to keep the emotion from her voice. "It sounds like he was miserable, and I applaud his courage in recognizing that and doing something about it. Can't your mom see that he's happier now?"

Laura's brows lifted, and she took off her shades. "You don't get it, do you? My mother doesn't want Ben to be happy. She wants him to be punished."

Katie drew back as though she'd been slapped. "Punished? What do you mean? Punished for what?"

The grin on Laura's face spread wide and slow, reminding Katie of Alice's Cheshire Cat. "Oh. I see. You don't know. He hasn't told you. Interesting." She looked back toward her brother and then sat up in a panic as she shouted, "Ben! What are you doing? I said not to go near the water."

"We're just rinsing his hands," Ben called back. "We're not going in."

Part of Katie wanted to latch onto Laura's arm and insist she tell her what the hell that meant before Ben got back within earshot. What was Ben not telling her? Why would his mother want him punished? For what? What had he done?

But a little voice kept chanting in the back of her mind

that this was none of her business, none of her concern. She was here for a week. Nothing more. Whatever Ben had done and whatever drama he had with his mother as a result was his problem to solve. She didn't need to know, and it would likely bring her nothing but misery to try and get involved.

Laura clucked her tongue against her teeth as she relaxed against the seat, standing down now that Ben and Brady were walking back towards the cabana.

"Did I not say to him that I didn't want Brady in the water? You heard me, right? I swear, no one in this family takes me seriously."

She sat up again and turned to put her feet between their chairs so she could lean in closer to Katie and whisper.

"You know what you and Ben need to do? You need to get pregnant as soon as possible."

Katie looked at Ben's sister like she'd sprouted a new set of feet from the top of her head. "What?"

"I'm serious," Laura said, laying her hand on Katie's arm. She glanced at her brother and son to gauge their closeness and then dropped her voice even lower. "It'll change everything. Mom hated Dale, but as soon as Brady was born, she was the happiest I've ever seen her. She's nice to Dale now, and she lets me do pretty much anything I want as long as she thinks it's Brady who wants it. He has her wrapped around his finger. Never underestimate how much leverage a grandchild can give you."

"That's horrible," Katie whispered, unable to stop the words from popping out.

"Oh, please." Laura waved away Katie's comment with a laugh. "It's the way things are. She controlled my father with us. I bet he never would have married her if she hadn't been pregnant with Ben, and he threatened to leave so many times, but there was always us to keep him there. As far as I'm concerned, she's reaping what she sowed, and I'm reaping the benefits of it."

"Mommy!" Brady yelled as he rushed to Laura's side. "Come and see the sandcastle Uncle Ben and I built. It has cannons pointed toward the water so we can shoot any ships that approach."

"Really?" She glared up at Ben. "Cannons? You know we're raising him to be anti-violence."

"It's an imaginary sandcastle with imaginary cannons to shoot at imaginary pirates," Ben said. "You and I built a thousand just like it when we were kids, and we didn't turn out violent."

"It's the point I'm making, Benjamin," she said, sounding eerily like their mother. "I expect you to respect my wishes if you're going to spend time with Brady."

"Of course," Ben said, his grin fading into the nothingness Katie had seen before around his family.

"I think I'm ready to head back to the boat," Katie said as she fought to maintain her composure and refrain from telling Ben's sister she was just as awful as their mother.

"Me too." He put his hands on his hips as he stared down at her. "I was thinking after we get cleaned up we could go back to that gelato place in the gallery and see if it's open. Maybe check out the chocolate shop, too?"

His eyes had softened when he looked at her, and his grin was trying to return.

She had another overwhelming urge to hug him, but this time it was because she wanted to wrap her arms around him and protect him from the vile nastiness he'd come from.

Despite her mind's protest, her heart carried forward. She stood and went to Ben, raising up on her toes to wind her arms around his neck and squeeze him to her, as though she really could shield him from the pain they'd caused.

She didn't know what he'd done or why he needed to be punished in his mother's eyes—or why his sister was okay with it—but in the short time she'd been around Ben and the even shorter time she'd spent with his mother and sister, she suspected she'd be on his side even if she knew.

Putting his arms around her waist, Ben held her as she clung to him.

"Wow," he said quietly against her ear. "That's quite the response. You must really like chocolate."

"Are you guys gonna kiss?" Brady asked. "Because that's gross, and I'm going to cover my eyes if you are."

"Brady!" Laura admonished. "What is with you and kissing lately? Did Grandma Jackson let you watch soap operas again?"

Reminded that they had an audience, Katie released her grip on Ben, but his arm remained firmly around her waist.

"You okay?" He said under his breath, his voice so quiet she barely heard him.

She nodded and pulled away, and his hand lingered on the bare skin of her back before he let it fall.

Laura had stood while they embraced, and she was watching them with her hand on top of Brady's head as he buried his face against her and said, "They're yucky."

"Don't mind him," she said to Ben and Katie. "Dale and I are always careful not to touch or kiss in front of him, but Dale's mom leaves the television on with the soap operas playing, and Brady's getting quite the education. I told Dale if she keeps it up, we're going to have to put our foot down and not let Brady go over there, but he won't stand up to his mom."

Ben chose not to acknowledge her comments and instead nodded toward the ship. "You guys heading back now? You wanna walk with us?"

"No, I better wait and see what Dale wants to do."

"All right then. We'll see you at dinner."

Sixteen

"I don't want to go to dinner with your family," Katie blurted out as they walked back to the ship.

"Please tell me what happened between you and my sister, and don't keep saying *nothing* and *it's fine*. Something happened, Kate. Your whole mood changed. Did Laura say something? Did she do something? I'm happy to go address it with her, but I need to know what she did."

Katie stopped walking and turned to face him. "I don't need you to go address it. I don't need you to do anything. It's fine, and I'm fine. But I don't wanna go to dinner with your family. I'll have dinner on my own."

She turned and continued toward the ship, and Ben stared after her for a moment before catching up easily with his longer stride.

"Okay, how about this? You jump in the shower, and I'll go grab a pizza from the little shop in the gallery. Then, we can sit out on the balcony and eat it before we head down to the beach party."

"I don't want to keep you from spending time with

them, okay? That's the whole reason you're on this cruise. I can get my own pizza. It's all right."

He grasped her hand and stopped walking, and when she stopped too, he attempted a smile. "What if I'd rather eat with you? What if I'd rather spend my time being Cruise Ben sharing a slice of pizza with Cruise Katie?"

Katie shook her head as she rubbed her lips together and then sighed.

How did she get so tangled up in this? And if she could see so clearly that she shouldn't be involved, why couldn't she just let go?

Pulling her hand from his, she crossed her arms over her bikini top. "What about Brady? You said you wanted all the time with him that you can get. Why skip a meal that he'll be at?"

"I make my memories with Brady, and the most special ones are never going to be around the dinner table with my mother."

The mention of his mother only stoked the storm brewing inside Katie. She wanted to ask him why his mother wanted him punished. What on earth could a son do that would make his mother actively work against his happiness? What could he have said or done when he was nineteen that couldn't be forgiven?

But if Ben wanted her to know, he clearly would have told her. Laura seemed surprised that he hadn't, and that told Katie he either didn't want her to know or he felt it had no bearing on their arrangement for the week. Either way, she wasn't going to ask and further insert herself where she didn't belong.

"You need to spend time with your family, Ben. They're going to be in your life a lot longer than I will."

She turned to go, trying to ignore how much it hurt to say that. But it was true. No matter how messed up Lydia and Laura were, and no matter how poorly they treated him, they were still his family. And she...she was a pretend girlfriend who had no stake at all to claim.

This time, Ben didn't try to stop her, and he offered no rebuttal as he stood there and let her walk away. He followed her at some point though, because she could feel his presence behind her, as though her body had already become attuned to know when he was near.

Neither of them spoke until they met up again while she was waiting for an elevator inside the ship.

"I need to take a shower," she said.

"Okay, sure. I'll, um, I'll go for a walk and give you some time to shower and change...and whatever else you need to do."

"I'll text you when I'm done."

She moved past him and started up the stairs, eager to burn off nervous energy and clear her mind of the wounded look on his face.

Being mean to him wasn't her intention, and hurting him was the last thing she wanted to do. Her anger wasn't even directed at him.

She was angry with Laura for being a slithering snake in the grass, whispering secrets behind Ben's back as she cheerfully plotted her manipulations.

She was furious with Lydia for being a nasty human being and for making Ben feel like he wasn't loved...or perhaps even lovable.

She was also mad at Maya, because she felt like she'd been sent out to sea without all the facts, and it hurt to think that her sister had been looking out for someone else's interests over her own.

But most of all, Katie was angry with herself. Once again, she'd met a guy and fallen for an idea of who he seemed to be. And maybe Ben was that guy, but there was no way for Katie to know. Because since the moment they'd met, she'd been snared in a web of omissions, lies, and deceit.

"Hey, how's the cruise?" Maya said when she answered the phone. "I can't believe you have a cell signal."

"Me either, and I don't know how long I'll have it or how much this is costing me to call you, so I need you to listen and I need answers.'"

"Okay. What's wrong, Kate?"

"Did you know Ben was interested in me before you said I should go on this cruise?"

"I knew he would like to get to know you better, yes."

"Oh my God, Maya. You set me up with your best friend without telling me!" Katie slapped her palm against her forehead as she paced the room wearing nothing but a towel. "Your best friend who has mother issues that are almost on a Norman Bates level. Your best friend who seems to loathe the family he was raised with and yet, for some reason I don't understand, he continues to submit himself to their craziness and abuse. Your best friend who is so witty, so smart, more handsome than any man should have the right to be and still be that nice. He loves to travel. He loves art. He loves movies. He's funny. He's creative. He's kind."

"I'm confused," Maya cut in. "Why are you angry but also telling me Ben's the perfect guy? What's going on? What happened? I threatened his life if he made a move on you, so please tell me I don't need to kill my best friend."

"You knew," Katie said, her voice shaking with anger. "You knew he was interested in me since that night at the concert. And you knew I had no idea who he was. He's been asking you about me for a year, Maya! Yet, you sent me in blind. I had no idea! Whose side are you on?"

"I'm not on anyone's side, Kate. But if I was, it would be yours. Every time. Period. What happened?"

Katie closed her eyes and focused on calming herself by exhaling out as much air as she could before slowing taking more in.

"Are you still there? Did I lose you? Kate?"

"I'm still here," Katie said. "I can't believe you set me up without telling me you were setting me up."

"I didn't! Christ, you were there when I fell off the ladder. Do you think I somehow did that on purpose just so I could get you to go on a cruise with Ben?"

"No, but me going was your idea. You knew he was interested, and you knew he would check every single box I've ever had for the type of guy I want to spend my life with. Oh, well, with one exception—his mother hates him and hates me by association, and she doesn't even know me! That's definitely not something I want to deal with for the rest of my life."

"Was she rude to you? Was she ugly to you? Did you say something? Ben better have stuck up for you. She has no right to be mean to you, Kate. Don't put up with that."

"So, does she have a right to be mean to Ben? What did he do, Maya? Because I know you know. I know you do. What on earth did this guy do to make his mother hate him so much? Did he murder someone? Is he a rapist?"

"Christ, Kate! What are you even saying? You think I'd send you on a cruise with someone like that?"

"I don't know. I feel like I don't know what anything is anymore. I don't know who or what to believe. Obviously, I don't know him. At this point, I don't even know who I am. All I know is I'm in a mess. I've fallen for someone who may or may not be real, and there are so many reasons I could give you why I shouldn't be with him...and you're one of them. But when I think of getting off this ship and walking away without him...this is ludicrous. I don't need this in my life right now. You knew that. You knew I was trying to get my life put back together. That I need to figure myself out. And you put me in this situation where you were, what? Hoping I'd fall in love with Ben and it would all work out so we could be one big happy family? You can't marry him, so you hoped I would?"

"Whoa. You are so far out of line right now, and you're saying crap that doesn't even make sense. Listen to me. I didn't set you up. The reason I didn't tell you he was interested is because you do need to figure yourself out and get your life together, and you just got out of a relationship. I'd be the last person to encourage you to rush into another. And might I remind you that even though it was my idea originally, I dropped the subject. You were the one who brought it back up, and you were the one who decided you wanted to go. I didn't push you into this. As far as Ben and his interest in you, I told him you needed this trip, and I asked him to take you. I thought it might help you break out of your funk and find some joy again. I hated seeing you without hope. But I wasn't kidding when I said I threatened his life if he made a move on you. I told him you were off-limits, so you better believe I'm gonna take it up with him if he—"

"That's not up to you. You can't control who I love and who loves me anymore than Ben's mom can control him. I gotta go."

"Wait. You never did tell me what happened."

"Ben," Katie said, closing her eyes again so it was easier to picture his smile. "Ben happened."

Seventeen

Once Katie was dressed and had dried her hair, she texted Ben that she was leaving the room so he could come and shower. Then, she wandered around the ship, lost in her own thoughts without any particular destination in mind.

She believed her sister was telling the truth. Maya may not have revealed all she'd known, but Katie didn't think she'd plotted to get her and Ben together.

She also had no doubt Maya had threatened Ben, and she wondered if that was why he seemed to hold back despite his obvious interest. It could also explain why he was more willing to be open with her when he was pretending to be a fictional character, though he was nuts if he thought Maya would let him off on that technicality.

Of course, then again, Katie could just be making excuses for Ben and trying to justify his actions—something she'd sworn she wouldn't do anymore after Grant.

As though she was on autopilot, she'd gone to the rear of the Lido Deck. It was packed with an evening crowd, and the domed seat where she and Ben had snuggled was taken.

Moving to the railing where they'd watched the moon, she looked out over Coconut Palms Cay. It was like a postcard with its white sandy beaches, swaying palm trees, and the vivid pastel and jewel-toned buildings the Caribbean was known for. The water surrounding the island had been a pale turquoise earlier when the sun was at its highest point, but now that its light had faded with it sinking toward the horizon, the waters had taken on a deep teal hue.

"I hoped I might find you here," Ben said as he came to stand beside her. "I tried to text you, but you didn't respond. I didn't know if that was because you didn't want to talk to me or because you didn't have a signal. I figured I'd find you and ask directly rather than making an assumption either way."

"I turned my phone off. I kind of, sort of hung up on Maya. I guarantee you I have at least ten voice mails by now telling me to pick up the phone."

Ben's lips formed an "O" with his exhale, but then he grinned. "I wouldn't be surprised if a helicopter lands on this ship and she jumps out of it looking for you."

"Yeah, neither would I." She refrained from telling him Maya would probably be looking for him too, but somehow, he guessed it.

Resting his forearms on the rail, he cocked his head to the side as he looked to her with a lifted a brow. "Should I be worried?"

"That she's going to come in a helicopter?"

"No. That she's going to come after me."

Katie turned to lean back against the railing so she could face him, but she'd misjudged how close he was.

The scent of his cologne washed over her in the breeze,

and her body reacted immediately before her mind could clamp it down.

"You tell me, Ben. Why would my sister be upset with you?"

"I suppose it depends on why the two of you talked."

"Do I need a reason to call my sister?"

He looked down at his foot as he tapped the toe of his leather sandal against the rail post, and then he straightened and shoved his hands in his pockets as his somber eyes met hers.

"No, but considering that you chose to do so from the middle of the Caribbean, I'm assuming you had a reason."

As she considered what to do with her predicament, she took a moment to just look at him.

His hair was damp from the shower, and though he'd combed it back, a few loose strands had fallen over his brow in the evening breeze. He'd changed into a pale ivory linen shirt with cuffs folded neatly against his forearms, and the brown cargo pants he wore fit slim through his hips. If he'd been standing on some random rock staring off into the distance, he'd have looked like a cologne model in a GQ magazine.

Her heart fluttered, and her body overruled her mind and began to burn for him.

"Did I do something to upset you, Kate? Did I say something to make you mad?"

She shook her head, biting down on her lip to keep from spewing out every thought she had.

He tilted his head again, bending slightly so they were almost eye to eye. "Now before I ask if that's your final answer, don't forget we have a rule. No lies between us."

She spun to face the island again, unable to continue staring into his eyes.

"Do you want me to leave you alone? Give you space?" he asked after a while when she didn't answer.

She ignored the voice in her head telling her to say yes and said no instead.

"Then tell me what's going on inside here, please." Ben tucked her hair back behind her ear as he gently tapped her head. "What did I do? I thought it was Laura because that's when everything changed, but I grilled the hell out of her, and she swears she didn't say anything. So, either she's lying —which, unfortunately, could be a possibility with my sister—or it's something I did."

"You didn't do anything." Which was true, for the most part. He'd made her fall for him when he was geographically unavailable, and he'd come along at a time in her life when she'd committed to do soul searching without another soul involved, but as far as her mood swing today, Ben had done nothing wrong—she'd just realized that it would never be right.

"Then what happened? We had a great day, didn't we? I thought you had fun. I had fun! I can't remember the last time I laughed that much or when I last felt that comfortable in my own skin. Maybe not ever."

"But it wasn't real." She turned to face him again. "I felt comfortable too, and yes, I had fun. Obviously. But I feel like I don't know how much of that is make-believe. Part of it? All of it? None of it? What's real? What can I trust? There is so much about you I don't know. And when we pretend we've already been together for years, it might be easier to kiss and hold hands without any awkwardness that way, but there's a lot we're skipping over. There's a reason it takes a long time to feel comfortable with someone. There's a reason it takes time to trust. I feel like there are things I don't know that maybe I should know. And at the same time, I feel like it's none of my business to ask, because, again, none of this is real. When we step off this ship in three days, you go back to your life, and I go back to mine. So does it even matter?"

He turned, leaning forward to brace his elbows on the rail as he stared down at the water lapping at the sides of the ship. "What do you wanna know?"

Everything, she wanted to say. What he was feeling in that moment. What he had carried forward from his past and what he wanted for his future. Why he looked at her sometimes like he wanted to devour her but then at other times like he was on the verge of crying.

She wanted to know what he felt when they touched, if he yearned for her the same as she did for him, and if he was just as conflicted as she was about the idea of a future together.

But what good would it do for Ben to bare his soul to her? Nothing he could say would change where he lived or who his best friend was or the fact that Katie had no idea what she wanted to do with her life. And it certainly wouldn't change how crazy his family was, though knowing the truth about what had happened might help her under-stand some of the *why*.

So, instead of saying *everything*, she said nothing.

"Please tell me what you want from me, Kate," he said after a while, shifting so his side was against the rail and he could face her again.

His eyes were dark with emotion but impossible to read. Was that fear? Hurt? Frustration?

Whatever it was, it wasn't joyful, and she was causing that pain.

Why put him through this when she already knew what the outcome had to be?

"An escape," she said, offering him a partial truth. "I want to escape with you. I want to laugh. I want to be happy. I want to forget there's a world we have to go back to at the end of all this. Can we just go play again?"

His gaze didn't waver, and his expression didn't change. She feared he was going to call her out for being dishonest. That he was going to tell her he knew she wanted more.

But he didn't. He just took her hand and started walking, and she had to wonder if that was because he knew it was hopeless, too.

After grabbing a pizza at the gallery, they left the ship to join the beach party already in progress. As a DJ blasted out reggae tunes, a group of revelers danced in the sand, while others played games led by the ship's entertainment crewmembers.

Lasers and spotlights filled the air around them with colors and shapes, and the entire vibe was so festive and fun that it was impossible not to feel lighter.

She didn't ask Ben what he'd told his family regarding dinner, and she tried not to feel guilty that he was with her instead of them.

She tried not to think about his family at all, or any other real-life obstacle she and Ben faced. Any time her mind drifted to doomsday plotting, as Ben had called it, she brought herself back to the present and focused on having fun.

They took the second-place ribbon in the three-legged

race, and then they danced to the *Electric Slide* and the *Macarena*. When the *Cuban Shuffle* music began, Katie motioned to Ben that she was thirsty, and they walked hand-in-hand in search of a bar.

With bottled waters in hand, they began to look for empty chairs along the beach.

"Those people look like they're leaving." Ben pointed to a couple who had just stood. "Not chairs though. It's one of those beanbag things. Is that okay with you?"

"Sure," Katie replied after chugging the last of her water. "I just need to sit down before my legs go out from under me. I had no idea it was such an aerobic workout to line dance in the sand."

Ben took her hand and led her to where the couple had departed, and then he plopped down on the beanbag, spreading his legs and patting the space between his knees. "C'mere. I want to hold you."

She turned her bottom toward him and eased her aching legs down, and once she was seated, she nestled into his arms, wriggling her rump back between his legs so she could rest her back on his chest.

"Is this okay?" she asked. "Are you comfortable?"

He tightened his arms around her, pulling her even closer, and then he nestled his nose against the soft skin of her neck just beneath her ear.

"Sweetheart, I am more than comfortable." He nibbled at her earlobe with a grin. "Why was I ever looking for chairs?"

She pulled her head away with a giggle, and then she rested it against his shoulder, turning so she could see his face.

"Happy?" he asked.

"Very."

With a feather-light touch, he reached to stroke his knuckles along the line of jaw, and then traced his thumb over her bottom lip.

Smiling as she shivered, he said, "I swear I could stare into your eyes forever and never tire of the view."

Her heart skipped a beat, her breath catching in her chest, but then she reminded herself that they were playing the game. "Why, thank you, Cruise Ben. What a lovely thing to say!"

She pressed her lips to his, and his hand cupped her face as he coaxed her to open up to him, deepening their kiss.

Every other time their lips had met as Cruise Katie and Ben, it had been pleasant, enticing, but tame. This was like nothing she'd ever experienced before, not even with the dizzying first kiss they'd shared in front of his mother.

His mouth was demanding and hungry, as though he couldn't get enough of her and feared she'd be taken away. She met his hunger with a ferocity of her own, twisting her upper body so that she could reach up and thread her fingers into his hair, clinging to him like her life depended on him.

As the tension they'd been holding at bay threatened to fully unfurl, they decided that a public beach might not be the ideal spot for them.

With a fevered urgency, they rushed back to the ship and made their way up to the room, barely able to keep their hands and lips to themselves along the way. At any opportunity when no other passengers were around in a hallway or the elevator, one of them would grab the other, and they'd be up against the wall, stoking the fires to keep them burning.

As soon as they crossed the threshold and the door had closed behind them, Ben put his arms around her waist and lifted her, their mouths never parting as he carried her to the bed and laid her upon it.

Lying down next to her, he pulled her into his arms, and then he brushed her hair back from her face and tucked it behind her ear as he rested his forehead against hers.

"Kate?"

"Yes?"

"Are you sure about this?"

Planting her hands in the center of his chest, she applied enough pressure to make him pull back without pushing him away.

"Are you?" she asked.

"Yes. God, yes." He took her hand in his and brought it to his lips. "But I need to know that you are, too."

She swallowed hard as she considered the question, running her fingers through his hair. She rested her hand on the back of his neck, and then took in a ragged breath.

"You asked me earlier what I wanted from you. Honesty. No more pretending. No alter-egos or fake personas to hide behind. If we do this, I need to know it's us. The real us."

His eyes were so intense that it was difficult to look into them without feeling overwhelming emotion. Or maybe she was already feeling it, and both of them were intense.

"I would be willing to give you whatever you wanted," he said, tucking his knuckle beneath her chin to lift her face to his. "My honesty, you already have. The only one pretending tonight was you. I never mentioned the game, or Cruise Katie and Ben. You asked me earlier how you can know what's real. It's been the real me by your side all night, and it's the real me lying here with you now. What I feel for you is real, Kate."

She had no idea if they could ever have a future, and she still worried about the things she didn't know from his past.

But New Katie was willing to live in the moment. She might not have him forever, but she had him for tonight.

EIGHTEEN

"Kate?"

There was that voice again, calling to rouse her from slumber.

"Kate?"

Soft lips gently kissed the back of her neck, and a strong hand moved over her ribs.

She smiled, recognizing the voice right away this time, as well as the lips and the touch of the hand.

"Yes, Ben?"

"It's time to get up, sweetheart." Another hand swept her hair aside as the lips trailed down her neck to nibble at her collarbone. "You have a St. Thomas history tour booked this morning."

"Ugh," she moaned, tossing her arm over her eyes as she dared to try and open them. "Can't we just stay in bed all day?"

Ben's chuckle rumbled in his chest, feeling like a nice vibration across her back. "Don't tempt me. I'll order room service in a heartbeat."

Shifting to lie on her back, Katie looked up at him

through sleepy lids. "That's not a bad idea. If we have breakfast delivered, then I have more time to lie here with you before I need to be at the gangway for my tour."

"All I want for breakfast is you," he said with a grin, and then he reached down and nipped her nose with a playful bite.

"Ow!" She moved to push him away, but he caught her hand and brought it to his lips.

"I didn't bite you hard enough to hurt."

"How do you know? If you're the one doing the biting, you can't feel the hurt of the bite."

"True," he said, half shrugging. "Here. Let me kiss it and make it better."

She closed her eyes as he came in close for the kiss, pressing his lips to the tip of her nose with the gentlest of pressure. Then he repeated the gesture by kissing each of her cheeks, and then brushing his lips against hers as he whispered, "Kate?"

"Yes?" Her breathy reply came as his lips grazed her forehead in a path of delicate, tiny kisses. She tilted her head forward to lean into him, wanting more of his tender touch.

Reaching to cup his hand behind her head, Ben pulled her in even closer as he planted a kiss between her brows. "I'm falling in love with you," he whispered against her skin.

She froze, her eyes popping open, and her breath held captive in her chest.

Then she rolled away from him and sat up to kneel on the bed.

"Oh, Ben. Don't do that."

"Don't do what?" He sat up against the headboard, looking at her in alarm. "What did I do?"

"Don't go there. Not now. Not this morning. Not today. We just had this incredible night, and I mean *incredible*...but it didn't magically erase all our problems."

"So?"

"So, you can't be in love with me. I can't be in love with you. We have too many strikes against us, babe. Too many mountains to climb. And if I start thinking about that, I'm gonna obsess over it. And then I'm going to be focused more on the disappointment than the joy, which we know Maya hates for us to do, and then I'll be in a funk the rest of the day. And I don't wanna be in a funk. I wanna be happy. I am happy. Even though we have to see your mother later."

Grinning after the last part, she leaned forward to give him a quick kiss before hopping off the bed. "I'm gonna jump in the shower."

"I can't stop what I'm feeling just because it's problematic, Kate."

She turned back from the bathroom and made a praying hands gesture under her chin.

"I really don't want to talk about this right now. We only have a limited amount of time to spend together before real life comes calling. I don't want to spend it worrying about what happens next. Let's just stay in the moment, okay? Let's just live for today. For right now. For whatever allows us to be together and be happy."

"Being in love with you makes me happy," Ben said with a grin. "In fact, I can't think of anything that makes me happier."

She returned to the bed to give him one more kiss because her heart was filled to overflowing, and the next thing she knew, they'd missed breakfast and her history tour. But she was okay with it, because she was positive she wouldn't have had more fun on the tour.

"I can't believe they want us to set up inside." Laura pressed her fingers to her temples. "I expressly told them I wanted the view of the water in the background of our pictures. How will anyone know we're celebrating Brady's birthday on St. Thomas if all the pictures I post are of some conference room that could be in Cleveland for all anyone knows?"

"What's wrong with Cleveland?" Dale asked. He'd been at the pool bar for a couple of hours before their taxi ride to the turtle conservation center, and he'd already walked down the street a half mile to reach a store and buy more booze.

Katie feared he'd be passed out by the time they sang *Happy Birthday*.

Ben looked up from playing rock, paper, scissors with Brady. "Why don't I go ask the coordinator if Dale and I can just move the table and chairs out here? She said the set-up crew works the night before so she doesn't have anyone on site to do it, but maybe she'd let us be her set-up crew."

"Dale has a bad back," Laura said, glaring at Ben with her arms crossed. "I can't have him out of work because she doesn't have her set-up crew on site on the day of a party."

"It's probably because it's a small party," Katie offered in explanation. "With only seven of us, they probably assumed there wouldn't be any extensive changes."

The glare Laura had directed at Ben was immediately redirected toward Katie, who clamped her mouth shut and decided not to open it for the rest of the day if possible. She'd already been barked at by Laura a couple of times, but she'd shrugged it off since Brady's mom was under stress trying to ensure he got the party she wanted.

"It shouldn't matter how big her party is," Lydia said without looking in Katie's direction. "Laura paid an exorbitant fee to have an event here. The least they could do is set it up where she wants it."

Katie's mouth was definitely staying shut on that one. So far, she'd avoided being the target of a Lydia attack today, and she wanted to keep it that way.

Not that Ben's mom was being nice to her or anything. Lydia just didn't acknowledge Katie's existence at all. She hadn't spoken to Katie, hadn't made eye contact with her one time during the whole outing, and if she did respond to or comment on something Katie said, it was directed to the air as if she were talking to no one. A few times, Katie had looked up to find Lydia staring at her and Ben, but the older woman would look away once she realized Katie knew.

She assumed Lydia was staring because she and Ben had been acting like teenagers, sneaking away to grab a kiss whenever possible, always touching in some manner if they were within two feet of each other, and laughing at inside jokes no one else seemed to get.

Since tossing aside all their pretenses and fake personas to acknowledge their feelings for one another, they were so focused on making the most of the time they had left together, that they didn't want to bother with worrying about anyone else.

Ben had even laughed a few times with his mother present, something even Laura seemed surprised to see him do.

Occasionally, Katie's brain would try and warn her of the potential pitfalls of going all in with Ben, but the way she saw it, she'd rather spend the time they had left on the cruise happy and in love than to be moping around overanalyzing and miserable. She knew she was due for a painful letdown once she got home and reality set in, but for today, she was blissfully content.

Having gone down a rabbit hole with her own train of thoughts, Katie was surprised to tune back in and realize they were still arguing over where to have the party.

"I thought it looked nice inside with the aquarium in the background," Dale said. "At least there's air conditioning in there. Who wants to be outside in the sun for a birthday party?"

"I didn't fly all the way to a godforsaken island in the middle of the Caribbean to be inside a conference room looking at an aquarium, Dale."

"I like the aquarium," said Brady, who had been ordered to sit at the picnic table nearest his mother and occupy himself with her phone, while the adults figured out the party.

"You can see aquariums back home," Laura said, her volume level rising in direct correlation with her frustration level.

"Hey, don't yell at him," Dale shouted. "It's his birthday, and by God, he oughta get to say where he wants to have it."

Laura flung her hands out with indignation. "He's five! He has no idea what's going to look great in pictures."

As she and Dale started arguing louder, Ben leaned in close to Katie.

"Hey, I'm gonna grab Dad and head inside to get the table. If not, we're gonna be out here yelling and screaming for the rest of the day. I'll be right back."

He planted a quick kiss on her lips, but then she grabbed his t-shirt with her hand and pulled him in for a slighter longer one. Grinning as she released him, she said, "Want me to come with you guys?"

Ben glanced over his shoulder at Brady, who had looked up from the phone and was watching his mom and dad argue.

"Nah. Why don't you keep an eye on the Braidster? If those two start going at it, maybe distract him with something. When they lose their tempers, they both get oblivious to who's watching and listening."

She nodded and then looked to Brady as Ben nudged his dad and the two of them left.

The little boy's mouth was pressed into a tight line, and his eyes were wide as he watched Dale and Laura debate who was right about inside or outside and everything in between.

Katie considered moving to sit beside Brady to keep him occupied, but that would put her in a front row seat much closer to the action. Her general viewpoint when anyone was arguing was to stay as far away as possible and refrain from doing anything to get noticed.

But it didn't take long at all for Laura to toss her mother an invitation to join the discussion, and once Lydia started telling Dale he was wrong, the situation escalated quickly.

Brady's chin had begun to quiver, and his eyes had turned glassy with tears.

"Hey, Brady," Katie called quietly, wanting to get his attention without drawing any to herself.

She motioned for Brady to come to her, and after a cautious glance toward his mom, he came scurrying over.

"Did you see that gigantic turtle over there?"

"Where?" he asked, immediately interested.

"Come see," she said, taking him by the hand. "I bet

this guy is really old. His shell looks like it's been around a while."

She walked him to the edge of the small courtyard where the party was to take place, and then she pointed out the large turtle who stood munching on some veggies on the other side of a low hedge.

"What do you think, Brady? Do you think he's old?"

As she'd hoped, the child began reciting all the facts he'd learned about tortoises and turtles, and for the moment, the heated argument behind him was forgotten.

"Look," Brady said, squatting beside the hedge. "He has a scar on his foot."

Katie looked back toward Brady's parents, but they were still engaged in a shouting match with his grand-mother, so she squatted next to him and asked what he thought had caused the animal's injury.

Suddenly, Laura screamed Brady's name at a blood curdling volume that made nearby birds take flight.

Katie stood immediately and waved to get Laura's attention. "He's over here. We found a tortoise."

Already sobbing, Laura came running over and fell to her knees, scooping Brady into her arms. Startled by the scream and his mother's tears, Brady began to cry.

"How many times have I told you not to run off?" Laura screamed at him. "How many times have I told you to stay by mommy? What if someone had taken you?"

"He was with me," Katie said. "It's my fault. I offered to help him find a turtle so he wouldn't be upset by you guys arguing."

"You had no right to take my child somewhere without my permission," Laura yelled at Katie while cradling Brady to her.

"I-I-I didn't take him anywhere," Katie stammered,

completely thrown by the level of Laura's vehemence. "He was upset that you and your husband were arguing in front of him. I was just trying to help."

"Don't you dare judge me!" Laura stood and moved Brady behind her. "You don't know my son. You don't know whether he's upset or not. You know nothing about my family."

"I wasn't judging you," Katie said as Lydia stepped closer to her daughter's side. "I just noticed that your son seemed to be bothered by his mom and dad arguing, as any kid would be, so I thought it might help if I distracted him until you two got things worked out."

"It was none of your business, and you had no right to take my son."

"Oh my God, I didn't take him! We were right here, literally steps away from you. You would have seen us if we hadn't squatted to get a better look at the turtle. I just didn't want him to be upset."

"He wasn't upset!"

"Yes, he was. Just like he's upset right now because you're yelling at me."

Lydia stepped forward with her arms crossed, and Laura immediately took Brady and retreated to the other side of the courtyard.

"My daughter doesn't need your help, and neither does my grandson. You aren't a member of this family. We don't even know you."

Katie took a deep breath and glanced toward the building, praying that Ben would return at any moment. The last thing she wanted was some kind of big showdown with his mother, and unease had begun creeping up her spine when she realized that Dale was gone and Laura was preoccupied with Brady, leaving her all alone with Lydia.

"I realize you don't know me, and I can see where it was upsetting for Laura to look up and not see Brady, but I had him. I wasn't going to let anything happen to him."

"Well, we don't know that, do we? All we know is that you're here with my son, and that in and of itself automatically makes you questionable."

"What? I don't know what your beef is with Ben, but —"

"Why are you here?" Lydia stepped forward, and Katie automatically tried to take a step back in response, but she was up against the hedge.

"What do you mean, why am I here? I came for Brady's birthday party."

"Who invited you? I certainly didn't, and neither did Laura. You're neither friend nor family, so you have no right to be here."

Katie had never in her life had someone attack her in such a manner, and she had no idea how to respond to it.

"I'm, uh, I'm sorry. I didn't...Ben invited me. He said—"

"If Ben invited you, it was only to piss me off and make things uncomfortable for everyone. It's a standard practice of his, and you are nothing more than the latest in a string of trollops he's used to get to me."

She stepped even closer, only inches from Katie, and despite knowing the hedge was right behind her, Katie tried stepping back again, momentarily wobbling as she struggled to maintain her balance against the hedge.

Katie wondered briefly if Lydia would assault her physically, but even the verbal assault was already too much to take. She looked to the building for any sign of Ben, even further alarmed to realize that Laura and Brady had gone. She was completely alone with this lunatic.

"I contacted my son's place of work in Barcelona when we got into port this morning," Lydia said with a twisted smile. "No one he's been working with for the last month has heard mention of a girlfriend or anyone named Kate. I also contacted several of his friends, and again, none of them had any knowledge of a girlfriend, and they'd never heard him speak of anyone named Kate. Or Katie, as you liked to be called. So, I don't know who you really are, and I don't know what gutter you crawled out of or what bar my son the addict picked you up in, but I do know you're a fake and a liar, whose life is so pathetic that you came on a cruise with a stranger and slept with him just because he enjoys embarrassing his mother. But guess what? The joke's on him. Because you're the one who looks embarrassed. Not me. You're nothing more than a trollop, and he'll dump you just as quickly as he dumps the rest."

Lydia stepped back, and Katie ran past her, the trees blurring with her tears. She ran past the building with Ben inside it, and past the private van they'd hired. She even kept running when she reached the road.

She didn't know where she was running to. She just knew she had to put as much distance as possible between her and that vile woman.

After crossing the main road, she ran through a parking lot toward a restaurant she saw in the distance. Her side cramped with a stitch that felt like a knife had been jammed between her ribs, but she continued to run.

The restaurant she'd aimed for was closed, but she saw a convenience store on the next block over, so she cut between the buildings to reach it.

She didn't realize until she'd burst into the store and doubled over holding her side that she'd left her purse and her cell phone on the table at the turtle center. Along with her heart, her dignity, and the man she thought she'd come to love.

Heaving in air and trying not to puke, she made her way to the ladies' restroom at the back of the store and locked the door behind her. Then, she let her back slide down it and buried her head in her hands to let herself cry.

Once her tears were spent and she was able to take a breath without the pain in her side, she stood and splashed her face with water. Then, she stared at her reflection in the mirror.

What just happened?

It was too much to comprehend. The attack. The nastiness. The insults and accusations. And the things Lydia had said about Ben. That he was an addict. That he purposely brought home people to embarrass Lydia. Women he found in bars.

Her first instinct was to think that none of it was true. It didn't go with the person she knew Ben to be, and it contradicted what her sister had told her of Ben.

But how well did Katie really know him? All she had to go on was who he presented himself to be. She knew what he wanted her to know.

Ben and Maya had both said he traveled a lot. Was it possible there were sides to him that Maya didn't see?

Covering her face with her hands, Katie shook her head.

No. No way. Maya was an excellent judge of character, and her sister knew Ben well.

And Katie might not have known him long, but she found it hard to believe she would feel such a strong connection and such deep feelings for him if he was as mean-spirited as Lydia had made him out to be.

Not to mention that Katie's personal interaction with

Lydia and her daughter made them much stronger contenders than Ben for people not to be trusted.

However, there was no denying that was the environment he was raised in. And if this was the mother who raised him, who knew what Ben was hiding?

Leaning back against the wall, she stared at the ceiling and sighed. She'd been so happy this morning. So filled with joy and hope for the day ahead. And now, she was stranded on an island with no identification, no money or credit cards, and no phone. And she wasn't about to go back to get them.

She knew Ben would look for her. She had no doubt. But did she even want to be found? Even if he was exactly who he said he was, how could there be any future for them if this was the family she'd have to deal with? No way would she ever want to see Lydia—or Laura—again.

But Ben...Ben was another story. And as the adrenaline rush began to leave her, and reality started to set in, her heart shattered with the loss of someone she'd never really had.

What had his mother told Ben when he realized Katie was gone? Would Lydia be honest about what happened? Would Laura be?

The conversation with Lydia kept replaying in her head, and each time, something different stood out.

She didn't want to believe anything Lydia had said, but she knew from the conversation with Laura that something had happened with Ben in the past. Katie had mentioned it on the phone with Maya, and Maya had skipped over it, neither questioning nor protesting the notion that Ben had done something his mother couldn't forgive.

Had Lydia been right when she said the only reason Ben invited Katie was to make them all uncomfortable?

She'd like to think that was a ridiculous notion, but this was a guy who had planned to allow Maya to come on the trip and pose as his girlfriend just so she could be obnoxious to Lydia.

He'd even said to Katie that he'd been looking forward to it.

And he'd made a point of calling Katie to discuss the party and make it sound like she'd be expected to attend.

Had he really put her in that position in hopes that it would screw with his mother and upset the day?

The sick feeling in her stomach moved into her chest, and she had to consider that maybe Ben wasn't at all who she thought he was.

"Kate?" Ben's voice called out through the door. "Kate, are you in there?"

He rattled the knob, and then pounded on the door.

"Laura told me what happened. She said Mother went after you. Kate, please, say something. Open the door. I know you're in there because the cashier said you went in and didn't come out. C'mon, sweetheart, please open the door and talk to me."

Sweetheart.

It had warmed her heart and made her giddy when he called her that this morning.

But now, it turned her stomach and made her puke up her lunch.

Nineteen

Once she'd emptied her stomach and washed her face, Katie unlocked the door. It wasn't like she could wait him out; he'd made it clear he wasn't going anywhere.

He rushed to pull her into his arms when she opened the door, and she didn't know whether she wanted to cling to him or push him away.

As more time had passed and she'd recovered from the shock and hurt of what had happened, she'd started to move into being outraged.

"Your mother is a lunatic," she said into Ben's shirt as he embraced her.

"Yes, I know," he said, pulling back to look at her. "Are you okay? Dumb question, I'm sure, but God, I was so scared I wouldn't be able to find you. You left your phone and your purse. I've got them here."

She grabbed them from him, and the relief she felt was so overwhelming she started to cry. She hadn't realized until that moment how scared she was about being stranded on the island with no way to call anyone to tell them where she was.

"Are you okay?" Ben tucked her hair back behind her ear and then wet a paper towel and dabbed at something on her shirt.

She didn't want to think about what it might be.

"Are you like in shock or something? Kate? Look at me. Talk to me, please."

"I want to go home."

"All right. Let me call a taxi to take us back to the ship."

"No. I'm not going back to the ship. I want to go home. To Maya's."

Ben looked stunned, and then even more concerned than he had before. His brow creased as he nodded. "Okay. I'll make the arrangements for us to fly out of here, but I'll need to go back to the ship to get our things and to let officials there know that we won't be continuing."

"I wanna go by myself."

Now, he looked like he was going to be the one breaking down.

"Kate, please. Please don't do this. Please don't shut me out. Please don't let her take you from me."

"What did you do?"

"What do you mean?"

Katie crossed her arms as she looked at him, trying to gauge whether he was the one she could trust. "What did you do to your mother to make her hate you so much?"

Ben flinched and sank back to lean against the wall. "Nice that you assume I did something."

"It's because I have no idea what happened. What else am I supposed to think? Your sister says that your mother doesn't want you to be happy. She wants you to be punished. Punished for what? Your mother says you're an addict who picks up women in bars and brings them home to embarrass her. Is that true?"

He swallowed as he looked down at his hands, and when he looked up at her, she was shocked to see his eyes filled with tears, his face contorted with pain.

No matter what doubts and fears she had, some part of her had fallen in love with the Ben she knew. And to see him hurting hurt her.

She went to him, wrapping her arms around his neck as he enveloped her in the tightest embrace she'd ever felt.

"Please don't go without me," he whispered against her hair. "I'll answer whatever you ask. I have no secrets from you, and I'll tell you no lies. All I ask if that you give me a chance to explain. And then, if you still want to walk away, I'll respect your wishes and wish you well."

Pulling away from his embrace, she reached up to run her fingers through her hair. "And if I don't give you a chance to explain, you aren't going to respect my wishes?"

A faint smile pulled at the corner of his lips. "No, I'll respect them either way."

"Can we talk somewhere other than this bathroom?"

"We can go wherever you'd like. But if we don't make it back to the ship before they set sail, all our belongings sail with it, and we'll likely pay a fine since this is a US port."

Katie scrunched up her lips as she considered her options. She'd already determined she didn't want to be stranded on St. Thomas. And the likelihood of finding a flight out tonight was slim to none.

Like it or not, her best bet was to go back to the ship for the night, and then catch a flight out of St. Maarten in the morning.

"All right. I'll go with you, and I'll listen to what you have to say. But I'm still going home tomorrow."

"Fine, but I'm not staying onboard without you. Will you let me take me you home? Your sister is probably going to kill me as it is, but at least let me bring you back to her in one piece like I promised."

Katie and Ben were both silent during the taxi ride back to the ship. She learned when she came through security that Ben had pretty much alerted the entire world to the fact that she was missing without her ID, wallet, or phone, so everyone at the checkpoint seemed relieved to see her safe.

The farther they got from what had happened, the more surreal it seemed.

Had Ben's mother really gotten in her face and accused her of being a trollop, of all things? Katie wasn't even sure she knew what a trollop was.

Ben could not have been more attentive on the way back to the ship and to their room. He seemed to constantly waver back and forth between wanting to hold her and wanting to give her space. And though she didn't say so, she was feeling much the same.

"I'm sorry, Kate," he said once they were back inside their room. "I never should've left you alone with her. I never dreamed she'd pounce like that, though. Laura said she thinks it's desperation...that Mother knows she's losing control. And my sister said to tell you she's aware she owes you an apology. She was distrau—"

"She needs to make her own apology, not pass it along through you."

"You're right, of course, and she did offer to apologize in person. Just so you know, I told Laura it was my idea to distract Brady. That you were just doing what I suggested, and that I would have done the same thing. She understands why you did what you did."

When Katie didn't respond, he continued.

"I should have protected you. I should have been better prepared. Hell, I should have never exposed you to them in the first place."

Katie smiled as her eyes welled up with tears.

"But then we never would have met."

"Something I'm sure you regret now, but I won't ever regret meeting you, Kate. No matter how this all turns out—and for the record, I hope it's together——I will always be grateful to have had the experience I had with you. The time may have been short, but I cherished every minute of it."

She couldn't think about that yet. It hurt too much to consider.

"I'd like to take a shower and wash the public restroom stench off me."

"Okay, sure, of course." He clasped his hands together and twisted them like he was nervous. "I'll go take a walk, and you can text me when you're done. You're not planning to bolt from the room as soon as I leave, are you?"

"You don't have to leave the room, Ben," she said with a half-formed grin. "We showered together this morning. I think I'll be fine with you being in the next room now."

When Katie came out of the bathroom in her pajamas after the shower, she was surprised to see that Ben had ordered room service.

"I didn't know if you might be hungry," he said, "but I figured you probably weren't going to be up for going to dinner." At the expression on her face, he rushed to clarify. "Not with my family. You don't ever have to see them again, even if by some miracle, we do stay together. I got nachos, since I know you like those, but no olives. And a pizza. Oh, and some chicken noodle soup in case you're still queasy. I know you were sick at the service station."

"I was sick because a crazy woman verbally assaulted me, and the guy I was falling for evidently has quite the colorful backstory he didn't see fit to share." She grabbed a pack of crackers and climbed onto the bed to sit cross-legged with her back against the headboard.

"I wasn't trying to hide anything from you. If you'd asked, I would have told you. We haven't really gotten around to the life history stage of our relationship yet."

"That's because we skipped ahead to be Cruise Ben and Cruise Katie. I told you all that stuff at the beginning is there for a reason."

The room grew silent except for the sound of Katie chewing a cracker.

"So," she said after swallowing the cracker and chasing it down with water, "are you gonna tell me or not?"

"I've already said I'll tell you everything, and I would have the other night before all this even happened. What do you want to know?"

"Are you an addict?"

"No. I went through a time in college where my recreational drug and alcohol use was out of control. But I quit cold turkey after a particularly devastating event in my life at the age of nineteen, which I'm certain you'll be hearing more about tonight. I haven't touched any drug or alcohol since then. Next question."

"Do you pick up women in bars and take them home to embarrass your mother?"

"No. Have I ever taken home a woman I've met in a

bar? Yes, of course, but to *my* home, not my mother's. I don't take anyone to meet my family. I told you that."

"You told me you don't take anyone you care about, because you don't want to see them treated unkindly. Which I have a whole new understanding of now."

"You are the first person I've introduced to my family since... Allison. Not that I've been in a serious relationship since then, but..."

"So why would your mother say that?"

"Because she's unhinged, and she hates me. There was one situation where I brought home someone I shouldn't have, and she's never forgotten it. But it didn't happen again."

Katie leaned forward, worried about what the next answer might bring. "Why does your mother hate you?"

"I think it started at birth when she realized motherhood was time-consuming and life-altering, and it wasn't going to be temporary."

"Seriously...what happened when you were nineteen?"

He stood and began to pace the room.

"I was a hellion as a teen, starting in high school. I put my parents through the wringer, and things only got worse in college. The summer I was nineteen, I started hanging out with an older woman, Gretchen. She was thirty at the time, and we had absolutely nothing in common except that we both liked getting high. Gretchen was a small-time dealer, which is how we met, and she threw killer parties. People of all ages and walks of life went to those parties.

"So, call it stupidity, or youth, or me being rebellious and hating my parents at the time, but I brought Gretchen home for dinner on a night when my parents were hosting a swanky dinner party—that's the one-time situation I was referencing. Gretchen was stoned out of her gourd and dressed like a hooker, and my mother was mortified and madder than I'd ever seen her. They kicked me out of the house that night, and for some reason, I thought it was a great idea to go stay with Gretchen."

He went to stand at the balcony door with his arm braced against the glass, and his forehead resting on his forearm.

"One night at one of Gretchen's parties, there was a girl named Henley. She was my age and beautiful. Real nice girl. I still to this day have no idea how she ended up at Gretchen's. She wasn't a regular. I would have remembered her, and afterward, no one seemed to know who brought her. I talked to her for a while early in the night. Like I said, she was beautiful, and I was nineteen. Gretchen and I were on the rocks. Let's be honest, I never really had romantic feelings for her. It was more of a...relationship of convenience, and staying with her day in and day out had made it less desirable." He lifted his head and looked back over his shoulder at Katie. "And let me stop to say, I'm not proud of who I was then or of the decisions I made. If I could go back and change them..."

He stopped for a moment, and when Katie realized he'd gotten choked up, she crawled to the foot of the bed to be closer to him.

"So, anyway." He cleared his throat and shook it off. "I'd been living with Gretchen for a few weeks, and I'd started looking for a way out, and she knew it. When she saw me talking to Henley that night, she went ballistic. Just blew up, yelling and screaming at me. She was jealous of Henley, and she knew I had one foot out the door already. So, we had this blow-up at the party in front of everybody, so folks knew Gretchen thought I was interested in Henley. I'd like to point out that nothing happened between me and Henley prior to that argument. I never saw her during that argument, nor did I see her at any point after it, not that I know of, anyway. You'll understand later why that's significant. Being upset with Gretchen and my general life situation, I got pretty messed up that night. The last memory I have was stumbling into the room I shared with Gretchen and crashing face down on the bed."

He paused, and Katie sensed that he was struggling with the memories he had to recall. She reached for his hand, and he jumped when she touched him, like he's gone somewhere else in his mind and was startled to see her there.

She gave a slight tug, and he sat on the edge of the bed, and then she sat next to him with his hand in hers.

Turning his head to her, he took in a deep breath, and her heart hurt to see the haunted look in his eyes.

"The next memory I have is of waking up in the back-seat of my car. I was groggy and nauseous, and I had no memory at all how I'd gotten there or why I was in my back-seat. It was a Camaro, and you may have noticed, I'm a tall guy. I don't fit in the backseat of a Camaro. But somehow, I was scrunched up in a ball laying back there. Henley was in the driver's seat. The car was running. We were parked on the side of the road, perfectly within the white lines of the paved shoulder. She was slumped against the driver's window, and I thought she must have passed out, so I sat up and called her name, and then I put my hand on her shoulder to shake her."

He drew in a jagged breath and let it out with a shudder as Katie tightened her grip on his hand. "She wasn't asleep, and she didn't wake up again."

TWENTY

Katie gasped, her hand flying to her mouth. "She was dead? How did she die?"

"They said she overdosed. But no one at the party saw her take anything. No one was willing to say if they saw someone give her anything. Nobody seemed to recall who she came with, and no one saw her leave with me. Or leave in my car."

"How could no one at a party see anything? Not one single person?"

"Obviously someone saw something, but not anything they were willing to testify about."

"Oh. Gotcha."

"So, as you might have deduced, it's not a great situation to be in when you wake up passed out in your car with a deceased person and no memory of what happened. Toxicology showed we had several of the same substances in our system, so it looked like we had partied together. And the one thing people at that party did seem to remember and were willing to testify about was my fight with Gretchen regarding Henley."

Ben looked at Katie, and she could see that it had taken a toll on him to share what he had. No wonder he hadn't told her. Who would want to voluntarily relive that to tell it?

"Did you get blamed for her death?"

He nodded, pulling his hand from hers to go and stand outside on the balcony.

Katie followed him outside, hugging her arms around her waist when she encountered the chilly air.

"What happened? Did you go to jail?"

"No." Ben sat in one of the chairs and then pulled the other one out to make it easier for Katie to sit in it. "I was never charged and never arrested. They never had enough evidence on me to make anything stick." He turned to look at her. "I didn't kill that girl, Katie. I used back then; I used a lot. But I never gave it to anyone else or turned anyone else onto it. That just wasn't my thing. I was out for self-destruction, not messing up other people. And the mixture that was in my system that night—the mixture in both of our systems—wasn't a combination I'd ever taken before. It also wasn't what I clearly remember taking when I got messed up before I went to bed."

"So, you think someone drugged you both?"

"I'm certain of it."

"Did they ever find out who?"

"No. I think Gretchen had an ax to grind with me and was jealous of Henley. I think she set me up to take the fall. She had access to every drug that was in our systems. She had access to my car keys. And the last place I remember being was passed out in her bed."

"Did the cops investigate her?"

"Yes, but they couldn't find enough to charge her. I always thought Gretchen was an informant, and I think she had someone high up that helped cover this up for her. But as you might imagine, it caused a lot of stress for my family. Nothing compared to what Henley's family went through, of course. At the time, my mother was a prominent figure in our community. She served on many boards and belonged to different leagues. She was well-respected, and her social status was—and is—important to her. She wasn't born into wealth like my father. It's something she fought for and went after, so achieving that status and being respected like that, it's a crucial part of her identity.

"When the media got ahold of the story, it blew up locally and to some extent on the statewide level. My mother couldn't leave the house without reporters, neighbors, friends, or strangers asking her to comment on the case. She pretty much had to step down from every position she held because of the publicity, the scrutiny, and just the general chaos surrounding our family. Everywhere you went in our town, everyone was talking about it. And they all had opinions, of course. On my guilt. My upbringing. Everything was under a magnifying glass." He paused for a moment and stood. "I'm gonna get a water. You want one?"

Katie shook her head and waited for him to return.

"Mother got to a point where she just wouldn't leave the house," he said when he sat back down. "For years. For any reason at all. Like, basically agoraphobic. She's better now, obviously, but she still doesn't like to be out in public. She hates crowds and feels easily overwhelmed in them. Henley lost her life, which is the greatest tragedy that happened that day. But in many ways, my mother lost the life she knew, and she's never really gotten it back. And she's never forgiven me for it."

"But if you were set up, then it wasn't your fault."

"She never believed I was set up, and that's because I'd lied to her so often, so I have no one to blame but myself."

Katie sat and digested all that he'd revealed. "Is that why you quit drinking? And the drugs?"

"Yeah. I was very lucky. Lucky to be alive that night. Lucky they didn't frame me well enough for it to stick. But also lucky that my parents were wealthy, and that my father, as one of the most successful attorneys in Northern California, had a lot of connections. It cost my parents a small fortune to get me through that with the best team money could buy. Then, my father called in every favor imaginable to make sure there was nothing on my record, and nothing that would keep me from going to law school. That had always been his dream. That I'd join the firm with him, and we'd be a team."

"So, that's why you went to law school."

"Yeah. I mean, it had always been the plan—their plan —but I'd bucked against it for years. I never wanted to be an attorney. Never wanted to be in a suit or sit behind a desk. But after that...after all they did for me, after all I put them through...I owed them my life. And my mother still reminds me of that every chance she gets."

"How did you make the decision to drop law and pursue your own dreams? That must have tough."

"It was near the end of my final year, and it all seemed so inevitable. Allison and I were engaged—again, someone else's plan for my life, not mine—and the job was lined up, the wedding was planned, she and my mother were shopping for houses, and I felt like I was drowning. For the first time since the night I woke up in that car, I wanted to use again. And I wasn't willing to go there. I wasn't willing to die, which I'm pretty sure would have happened if I'd ventured down that path again. So, I dropped out, called off my wedding, packed up my car and took off. I went in search of a place to belong. Somewhere I could finally be me. I had some incredible experiences, and I learned a lot about people and the world. And it turns out what I was looking for didn't exist at any destination. It was a place I had to find inside here."

He bumped the bottom of the water bottle against his head.

"Like I said when you asked me before, I didn't give up a legal career to *become* an artist. I *am* an artist. Always have been and always will be. I'd just always been told that wasn't a viable path for me. It has taken me years to accept who I am and who I was. To forgive myself where I can for the mistakes I made, and to try not to punish myself too harshly where I can't forgive me yet.

"But in my mother's eyes, I walked out on a debt and left it unpaid. She'd determined a path for me. Her path for me. And I think she felt that my success on that path would have helped restore her and redeem her in the eyes of those who had judged her for my failings. Being an attorney at my dad's firm was on that path. Marrying Allison, or rather marrying into Allison's family, was on the path."

He grew quiet, and Katie allowed him the space to sit in silence, listening to the waves. After a while, he turned up the water bottle and drained it.

"I wasn't joking when I said Lydia hates me for being born. She also hates me for being an embarrassment in the years prior to Henley's death, and for robbing her of the life she'd worked so hard to achieve because of a scandal I brought to her doorstep. I tried to take responsibility for that. I swear, I tried to do the right thing by her. To make it up to her and to my father for what I'd put them through. But it was never enough. She was never going to forgive me, and I wasn't living my life. I was living in penance instead. Never-ending penance. So, when I made the decision to break free and live for me, my mother vowed she'd spend the rest of her life punishing me until I got back in line and back on the path. It's why she can't stop with Allison. She's still holding onto the idea that if she could just get me in line, she'll get all the things she deserves. The things I robbed her of." He leaned forward to rest his elbows on his knees as the stared into the water. "She's kept her promise so far. She's tenacious, I'll give her that. I can't tell you what all she's done to me, and what she's ruined in my life."

Katie sat up and leaned forward to look at him. "So, why is she still in your life? Why on earth would you ever go to a family dinner with her? Or go on a cruise? Oh my God, that's insane. You're insane. Well, she's insane, but why do you put yourself through that?"

"I think part of it is that—despite years of therapy—I believe I still deserve to be punished on some level. I mean, ultimately, whether I was set up or not, what happened to me and my family was my fault. I made some bad choices back then. And living with that is something I've worked on and continue to work on." Shifting to sit up straight, he said, "I also was telling you the truth when I say that I do it for Brady. I can already see in my sister that she's going to be a clone of the woman who raised us, though I must admit, I was pleased to see that Laura did the right thing today. When she realized what was happening, she came and got me, but it was too late. You were already gone."

"I watched for you," Katie said. "Not that I want to be that kind of girl who needs to be rescued, but no one had ever talked to me like that. I felt like I was under attack, and for someone who has always been the golden child who could do no wrong...well, I didn't know what to do with so much venom directed my way. She said I wasn't invited and had no right to be there. She called your gallery in Barcelona. Called your friends, though I don't know who. They all verified that you didn't have a girlfriend, and no one knew who Katie was. She said my life was pathetic because I came on this cruise and slept with you and agreed to live a lie. What could I even say to that?"

Ben rose from the chair so quickly that it clattered against the balcony wall. He knelt before her, laying his hands on her thighs. "Don't let her in your head. Don't let her poison work its way into your bloodstream. I've been trying for years to heal the damage she's done to me, and I still struggle with feeling unworthy of love. Not to mention being scared to let anyone in my heart knowing this is the kind of thing they'll have to deal with. You were invited. Laura called me months ago and said to bring my friend. I hate that I didn't come to your rescue. I hate that she attacked you because she saw what you mean to me. I'm sorry. I don't know what to do. I don't know how to fix this and get back to where we were before."

A solitary tear rolled down Katie's cheek, and he reached to wipe it away with his thumb.

"I love you," he whispered. "I don't want that to be a bad thing."

"I don't either, but I don't know what to do. This is a lot, Ben. This day has been a lot."

"I know. What can I do? Tell me, and I'll do it. I want to make it right. I want to make it okay."

Another tear threatened to fall, and Katie swiped at it, looking up toward the sky and away from Ben's pleading eyes. "How's Brady? Is he okay? The poor kid's probably traumatized. He'll never want to have a birthday party again."

"He's okay. Unfortunately, it's not the first time he's seen things go south. I wanna be around for that kid. I wanna be someone who will stick up for him, advocate for him. I want him to know he has someone he can turn to. That's something I never had, and if I can maintain some type of relationship with Brady and help him get to adulthood without screwing up as badly as I did, then I reasoned it was worth what I had to go through seeing my mother a handful of times in the year."

Katie was unable to even conceive of seeing that woman again. She could understand his commitment to Brady, and she felt sorry for the little boy, but if Lydia was going to be a part of Ben's life, Katie couldn't be. And she could never ask him to make such a choice.

"I'm tired," she said "I'm gonna get some sleep."

Ben rose with her and took her hand, pressing his lips to the inside of her palm. "I'll take the floor if you want, but if I could, I'd really just like to hold you."

Katie nodded without any hesitation, wanting and needing the same. She didn't know what tomorrow would bring, and she was still determined to get off this ship first thing in the morning. But she chose to be in the present, loving Ben and being loved in his arms.

TWENTY-ONE

Katie sat on the edge of the sofa and waited for Ben to stir. He looked so peaceful, lying there on his side with the sun streaming across the sheets.

They'd held each other all night, but then she'd eased herself away from his embrace once she woke. And now, she sat waiting with her heart in her throat.

As though he sensed her stare, Ben's eyes fluttered open, and then once he found her in the room, he smiled. "Good morning. You okay? You're already dressed."

He spied the suitcase by the door and sat up, rubbing his face with his hands. "What's going on? What time is it?"

"It's almost nine. They should be giving the all-clear to disembark in St. Maarten soon. I got a signal on my phone and booked a flight. I fly out at noon."

He lay back down with his arm flung across his forehead, the sheet dangerously low across his hips.

She looked away, not wanting to remember all the ways they'd explored each other's bodies. Not now. She'd have plenty of time to replay that over and over in her head once he was gone.

"I want you to know that I'm not leaving because of anything you told me last night," she said, her voice unsteady though she'd rehearsed this speech mentally at least a hundred times since she woke. "And I'm not leaving because of what happened yesterday...well, not entirely, anyway. What I meant was, I'm not leaving because of your mother. I'm leaving because of me. Because I need to figure out who I am and what I want. I need to learn how to be as strong as you were and be willing to choose my own path no matter what other people want me to do."

He moved his arm from his eyes to look over at her when she paused, and her breath caught in her throat when their gazes met.

"I need you to know that it's incredibly difficult for me to walk away. I've never felt the way I feel with you, Ben, and no matter what happens, I will always cherish every single minute of loving you and being loved by you. But this all came on so fast and so strong, and I'm not ready. I have a lot of work to do on myself. I have no idea where I'm heading or what I'm doing, and I have, and I have to *find* my path before I can ask someone to walk it with me."

He moved to sit up, wrapping the sheet more tightly around his hips.

"I'll wait. I don't care how long it takes. I know I want a life with you, Kate, so whenever you're ready, whenever you figure out where that path is heading, you just let me know. I'll be there to walk it with you."

She looked down at her hands, unfolding and folding the tissue that was damp from her tears, and her voice trembled when she spoke.

"I don't want you to wait. I'm not asking that of you. I have no idea what the future holds for either of us, but I would never want you to put your life on hold for me.

You've already lived in shackles far too long. I don't want you shackled to me."

Coming to kneel in front of her, he took her hands in his. "That's not how I see it. You have no idea how many ways you've set me free, Kate. What I feel for you, what I experience when I'm with you, I didn't think I would ever be allowed to have this."

"But you deserve it, you beautiful man," her voice choked as she pulled her hands free to cup his face. "You deserve so much love, and you should be able to give it and receive it freely. You shouldn't have to wait for anyone. Please don't keep yourself closed off from love any longer, and don't waste another day missing out on love because of me. Promise me you'll put yourself out there. Promise me you won't wait around for me. Because I have no idea where I'm headed, Ben. And I can't figure that out if I'm trying to keep you with me."

He pulled back from her hands, his jaw tight as he rubbed at the moisture in his eyes with a frustrated fist. "You're going to tell me we can't keep in touch, aren't you? You're going to cut me off completely, aren't you?"

"I can't keep one foot in this and one foot out. It's killing me to let you go, but if I don't, how will I ever know if I'm making decisions for us or for me? I need to find my way on my own. And so do you. I want you to be happy too, you know."

He stood and went to the glass door, staring out at St. Maarten, and then he took a deep breath and let it out with a slow, audible exhale.

"Kate, the first time our paths crossed, I regretted that I didn't try harder. That I let you go without at least making an effort. And now, our paths have crossed again, and I told myself I wouldn't make the same mistake twice." He looked over his shoulder at her and then turned to face her. "Every instinct I have is telling me to fight for you. To beg you to stay and give me a chance to prove this can work. That we can work. That we can build a future together and find our path together. But I also want to respect what you're asking of me and where you're at. I know what it feels like when you need to stand on your own and figure out where you want to go without anyone else's influence."

He came to kneel in front of her again, and then he made an effort to smile.

"I want you to be happy. I want you to be the best and most healthy version of yourself that you can be. And if that means I have to let you go for now, then I will."

Her heart clenched. He'd given her what she asked for and what she needed, but it wasn't at all what she wanted.

Throwing her arms around him, she pressed herself to him, holding on as tight as possible as she prayed for the strength to let go.

He wrapped his arms around her and held her just as tightly, his face buried in her hair.

Then he released her and stood, pulling her up with him.

After brushing the hair back from her face, he wiped her tears as best as he could, and then he pressed his lips to her forehead, cradling the back of her head in his hand.

"Our paths have crossed twice now," he whispered, his lips never leaving her skin. "I choose to believe they'll cross again when the time is right, and then they'll merge and become one path."

He tried again to smile as he pulled back to look at her. "You go forth and find your best life, Kate. I won't stand in your way, but I'll always be ready and willing, waiting for you."

Twenty-Two
Six Months Later

"You almost done?" Maya asked as she stood in the door frame of Katie's bedroom. "I need to talk to you about something."

"Yeah, just let me get this last paragraph finished, and that way, I can start on the epilogue tomorrow."

"And then I get to read it?"

"How do you expect me to finish the last paragraph with you hovering and asking me questions?"

"All right, all right," Maya held up both hands with a grin. "I'll meet you in the kitchen."

Katie joined her a few minutes later, taking a seat at the table and grabbing a tangerine from the bowl in the center. "What's up?"

"I have something I need to tell you, and I'm not sure how you're going to react. I choose to believe it's positive news, but I can acknowledge that your feelings may be different from mine."

"Are you getting back together with Danielle? We talked about this. If she can't make time with you a priority in her life, then she has to go." Katie finished peeling the tangerine and popped a wedge in her mouth.

"No, it's not about Danielle. Although she did call yesterday so it's weird you mention her. It's about Ben Reyes."

Katie stopped chewing for a split second as she absorbed the name, but then she continued and swallowed like nothing had ever happened. "I love the way you say his first and last name. Like I wouldn't know who you were talking about if you just said Ben."

Maya grunted. "Who knows? Maybe you forgot about him already. That's what you were trying to do, right?"

"I was never trying to forget Ben, Maya. It's not like I could, even if I tried."

"All right, well, like I said I don't know how this is going to go over, but I invited him to attend the dedication ceremony next week for the new storefront."

Katie's heart leapt at the thought of seeing Ben again, but outwardly, she lifted her shoulder in indifference and popped another tangerine wedge in her mouth. "Okay," she said around it. "I appreciate you letting me know."

Maya raised both brows and made a grand gesture of looking around the room in surprise. "That's it? You're not upset? I'm happy about this, obviously, but I really thought that telling you you're about to see Ben for the first time since the cruise would get more of a reaction."

"Sorry to disappoint, but I've been expecting this news ever since you told me that he's our generous benefactor, which I still can't believe you kept from me for months."

"What was I supposed to do? You spent two weeks without leaving your bed when you came home from that cruise. I've never seen you cry that much in my life. You were over Grant in, like, a day. So, yeah, once you started to be semi-normal again and decided you wanted to stay on with me and help manage the shop, I wasn't about to tell you Ben was my silent partner and risk sending you into a spiral."

"I get why you didn't tell me, okay? It just hurt when it felt like you'd kept it a secret. And it bothered me to think that I was connected to him through work when I'd tried so hard to move on without him."

"Are you going to be okay seeing him? It seems like you've been in a good place lately, mentally and emotionally. I think writing again has helped."

"Oh, for sure. And yeah. I'm good. Really good. I feel like I have a good grasp of where I'm headed. I know now what I want for my life, and I might not be able to have it all, but it feels good to have clarity about what it is."

"Good. I'm happy for you. It makes my heart smile to see you happy. I love you. You know that, right?"

"For sure. Love right back at ya."

Katie was a bundle of nerves arriving at the new storefront for the dedication ceremony. She'd thought about calling Ben and asking if he wanted to meet for coffee before the ceremony so there wouldn't be any awkwardness between them to mar Maya's celebration.

But in the end, she'd chickened out.

She had no idea what was going on in his life now, having demanded that Maya not breathe a word of him after she returned from the cruise. She wondered if he'd found someone. If he'd found happiness after she let him go. Had he extended in Barcelona or had he moved onto some other exotic locale? Perhaps he'd even come back here like he said he might do, but Katie felt like she would have known if Ben was living right down the street. She was certain she would have felt him nearby. That fate would have drawn them together at the grocery store by now.

No, he was likely flying in just for the ceremony. Best to wait and see how things would go when they saw each other, rather than calling and forcing fate's hand.

She scanned the gathering crowd, eager for any sign of him, and as she had before at the airport in Miami, she spotted him before he saw her.

Goosebumps rippled across her skin, and her heart rate soared as she saw the man who lived in her dreams standing across the street.

His hair was slightly longer—nothing like the Alaskan Wildman she first met—but long enough that it brushed the collar of his shirt. He was tanner than she remembered, and as he looked both ways and started across the street, her mind inundated her with flashbacks of his smile, his kiss, his touch, his love.

She wanted to run to him. To throw her arms around his neck and wrap her legs around his hips and tell him how happy she was to see him.

But somehow, she managed to refrain, choosing only to step forward when he grew closer.

The moment their eyes made contact, the connection was there, just as strong and powerful as it had ever been.

She smiled, and so did he, and then she moved forward through the crowd to meet him halfway.

"Hi," she said, biting her tongue to keep her heart from flowing out of her mouth in words.

"Hi." His eyes swept over her in the quickest of appraisals, and then they locked with hers again. "You look great."

"You too."

They both chuckled at the awkwardness, and then he said, "Congratulations on the opening. Maya told me you've decided to stay on with her and help run the shop. She's really happy about that. And yoga! Wow. She said you're getting certified as an instructor. That's cool."

Katie silently cursed her sister for being such a blabbermouth, but she couldn't help wondering if Maya had volunteered the information or if Ben had asked. She'd begged him to move on. To get on with his life and not wait for her. Had he done as she asked?

"Yeah, I'm excited about both. Thanks. How about you? What are you up to? Still in Barcelona?"

"No, I, um, I chose not to extend. I've been spending some time in Paris with a friend and now, I'm...well, I'm back here for a while. Just got in last night, in fact."

Katie's mind had zeroed in on the word *friend*, and she wondered what he might mean by it this time. Was it truly a friend, or someone more intimate? She had given up the right to ask.

"Paris! It's on my list. I'll make it there someday."

"You'd love it."

He smiled, and though it wasn't the one that always set her on fire, it was enough to make her feel like the sun was shining brighter and hotter than before.

"I, um, I have to go and help out with getting things ready for the ceremony," she said, pointing her thumb over her shoulder.

"Of course, yeah." He nodded and seemed to step back a little, as if to give her space. "Don't let me keep you from what you need to do. It was great seeing you, Kate. You look happy, and happiness looks good on you."

She wished she could know where he was with his life.

If he'd moved on, she needed to let him. But there was something there. Something in the way he looked at her. So, she took a chance.

"Would you, um, would you be available to stick around after the ceremony? I have something I'd like to show you."

His eyes lit up, and there was no mistaking that he was pleased by her request.

"Of course. Yeah. I'll be here. I'll wait."

She wondered if he'd chosen those words on purpose, and if they still meant what they had. She supposed she'd find out soon enough.

"Hey," Katie said to Maya as they finished cleaning up once the ceremony was done. "I'm going to be a little late to the reception. I have something I want to show Ben, so I'm gonna head back to the house with him, and then I'll come to the restaurant, okay?"

Maya's eyes widened, and she blinked a couple times. "Okay. Yeah. Whatever you need to do. Is everything all right?"

"Yeah. It's good. I just wanted to show him the book. Let him know I've been writing. Unless you've already told him that too," she said, giving her sister a playful glare.

"I only told him things about your life that are directly related to the store. He is my business partner, so I let him know that I had hired you to be a manager, and that we planned to go ahead and convert the conference room for yoga classes. I said you were being certified to teach them. I told him nothing more."

"It's okay," Katie said, smiling at her sister.

"I must admit I'm a little hurt that you're showing him the book when I haven't read it yet." Maya grinned. "I'm assuming you have your reasons, and that you know what you're doing."

"I do have my reasons, and I know what I'm doing. I just don't know how it's going to turn out."

Maya put her hands on Katie's shoulders and rested her forehead against her sister's. "Follow your heart, and trust that the best possible outcome will happen. Whatever that may be."

Katie thanked her and turned to go, and then she looked back to Maya. "Hey...is he dating anyone?"

Maya's grin was sly and knowing. "I thought you said I wasn't allowed to tell you anything about his life."

"Oh, for God's sake, Maya. I don't want to interfere if he's happy...if he's moved on. Just tell me."

Maya's grin faded with the understanding of Katie's fears.

"He waited, Kate. Like he told you he would. There's no one else."

"The place looks good," Ben said as he stood in Maya's kitchen, waiting for Katie to pour their iced tea. "How's Maya as a roommate?"

"Better than she was in high school, that's for sure. She at least picks up her own clothes now. Though she still leaves the dishes in the sink."

Once they'd settled on the couch, Katie rubbed her palms over her skirt, trying to find the courage to say what needed to be said.

"I want to thank you for giving me the space I needed.

I've done a lot of soul-searching, and I've made a lot of decisions about my life. Mainly, I've decided to be happy. To fill my life with things that bring me joy. The beach does that, so I plan to stay here. Maya brings me joy, and I think we were both surprised to find how much we enjoyed working together. I'd never really had fun at a job before, and I have that being at the store with her. I also weirdly enjoy the accounting part, which I'm sure you know she sucks at."

"That I definitely know," Ben said with a grin.

"Yoga brings me peace, and it helps me find my inner thoughts and listen to my own heart. Since I knew Maya wanted to convert the space and hire a teacher, I decided to get certified so maybe I can help others find that same calmness. I'm looking forward to that."

He rested his elbow on the back of the sofa and propped his head on his hand. "It sounds like you're doing great. Like you're finding your way. That's awesome. I'm glad things are working out for you."

"My mother hasn't been thrilled with my choices, but I'm learning how to separate my needs from hers and set healthy boundaries. And she's learning how to honor them, for the most part. I think the improvements in my relationship with Mom have started to help her relationship with Maya, so that's been a nice bonus."

"Maya mentioned that she and her mom have been getting along better. I'm glad all are you are moving forward in a healthy way."

"What about you?" Katie said, hating to bring up his mom, but wanting to know how he was doing with that. "How's Lydia?"

He stiffened slightly, but nothing like he'd done before when the topic of her came up. "I cut all ties with her after St. Thomas. I went zero contact, and it's been much healthier for me. I still correspond with Laura, and I'm able to see Brady and interact with him, so I'm happy about that. And my dad and I meet up now and then. So, things being what they are, they're good. Thanks for asking."

"So, I said I wanted to show you something, and I'm a little nervous about that." She rubbed her palms up and down her legs as she smiled. "I haven't shown anyone else, and when Maya told me you were coming today, I felt like I wanted you to be the first to see it."

His brow creased with a bit of confusion as he smiled. "Okay. I'm very curious as to what this is, but I'm also concerned. If you're this nervous, should I be nervous too?"

"I don't know. I don't know how you're going to react."

"Okay." He said up, rubbing his hands together as though he was eager, and then he gave her a nod. "I'm nervous, but I'm ready. Give it to me. Whaddya got?"

She went to her room and retrieved her computer, and then she opened the file and turned the screen around to show him.

"I wrote a book."

His eyes lit up as they widened, and his smile filled his face. "Really? Oh my God, Kate. That's great."

She handed him the laptop so he could take a closer look and then confusion returned to his eyes. "*Moonlight on the Lido Deck*? That's the title?"

Kate nodded and took a deep breath, preparing herself to reveal her heart.

"It's about a girl who meets a guy on a cruise ship. And out of nowhere, they fall in love. It happens so quickly that neither of them knows what to do with it, and they both have lives and responsibilities back home. But love doesn't really care what you have planned, and it doesn't care about what it's supposed to do or not do. Love just is. So under a full moon on a star-filled night, they sit in a half-domed chair and promise that whatever comes, they'll stay together and figure it all out."

Ben's smile trembled a bit, his mouth opening and closing as he processed her words. "Does it end in a happily ever after?"

"Of course. A true romance must have a happily ever after. It's in the definition of the genre. Go ahead and scroll down farther. There's something else I want you to see."

"I can't believe you wrote a whole book since I last saw you," he said as he moved his index finger across the mouse pad.

"You gave me back my creativity, Ben. When you and I came up with those characters and those stories and scenarios on the ship, it reminded me how much fun it is to pretend. It brought back my love for coming up with stories, and I can't thank you enough for that gift."

He stopped scrolling and looked up at her, his eyes misty. "You named the hero Ben?"

She shrugged with a tentative smile. "Yeah. It was what Cruise Katie did with her Italian book, so it only seemed fair. I may change it though. You know. Make it more of a fictional character. He was Ben in my head when I was writing. He was...you. There's something else though. You must have scrolled past it."

Leaning over closer to him, she reached across and scrolled back until she found it.

"There. The dedication. Read it aloud."

His eyes met hers, and then he looked to the screen and began to read.

For Ben.
    I found my path.
    Now I'm ready and willing, waiting for you.

The computer was set aside and forgotten, and they missed Maya's party too. But Katie knew her sister wouldn't mind, because Katie was living in the moment, enjoying the best possible outcome.

EPILOGUE

Katie put a hand on either side at the bottom of the window and pulled with all her might, shimmying the old, warped wood back and forth to get it to move up its track.

"Hey babe," she called, hanging her head outside to look down on Ben in the courtyard. "I've got lunch on the table. You ready to come in for a bit?"

"I just need another minute. Be right up."

She smiled and turned to walk back to their kitchen, reaching to grab a grape from the charcuterie platter on the table and popping it in her mouth. She noticed that the sink was dripping again, and she made a mental note to have Ben work with her so she could remind the landlord to fix it in Italian.

At the sound of Ben's feet on the stairs, she pulled the bread from the oven, wincing as the heat blasted her face.

"How's it coming?" he asked once he'd kissed her. "Did you figure out the scene that was giving you fits?"

"I think so." She sat in the chair he held out for her. "I don't know. I worry I'm introducing too many characters."

"You need to trust yourself, sweetheart. Your readers have loved all your other books, and they'll love this one too."

"I hope so. Maybe when you finish painting for the day, I'll read the scene to you, and you can tell me what you think."

"I'm finished."

She looked up at him in shock. "What? Already? You're not working this afternoon?"

"I finished the painting, Kate."

"Ben! Why didn't you tell me? I can see it now, right? You said I could see it as soon as it was done." She jumped up and moved to sit in his lap. "When can I see it?"

He smiled as he wrapped his arms around her and gave her a quick kiss. "I'll take you down and show you as soon as we finish eating."

"No way!" She stood and motioned for him to come. "I can't possibly eat now, knowing it's done. C'mon. I want to see it. Show me now!"

Laughing, Ben took her hand and let her down the stairs and into the small courtyard of the Italian villa they were renting for the summer. He told her to stay where she was, and then he walked around the small fountain in the center of the courtyard and turned the easel so that the painting faced her.

Katie gasped in delight, her hand trembling as she covered her mouth and began to laugh. She walked forward and peered at the intricate details Ben had captured of the quaint courtyard with its potted flowers and bubbling fountain. And then she looked at the woman sitting on the edge of the fountain, dipping her toes in the water as she tossed her head back and laughed, the joy in her face so radiant that it seemed to leap off the canvas and touch Katie's heart.

"You put me in your painting!"

Ben grinned as he stood behind her, pulling her back into his embrace as he rested his chin on her shoulder. "It was only fair. You put me in your book. Now we're just like Cruise Ben and Cruise Katie."

Turning in his arms, Katie smiled up at the man she'd chosen to live her life beside. "We're so much better than Cruise Ben and Cruise Katie, babe. We found a happily ever after in real life. What could be better than that?"

I hope you enjoy cruising with Katie and Ben! If you'd like to check out more of my stories, you can find them at www.violethowe.com!

And if you're not ready to leave the beautiful Caribbean yet, you're in luck—the next ship in the Sail Away Series is also embarking on a Caribbean cruise! Continue your Caribbean tour with Gabby in The Winning Tickets, Sail Away Series Book 7, by author Judith Keim.

★ **Don't miss a Sail Away book!** ★

Book 1: Welcome Aboard – prologue book
Book 2: The Sound of the Sea by Jessie Newton
Book 3: Uncharted Waters by Tammy L. Grace
Book 4: A Not So Distant Shore by Ev Bishop
Book 5: Caroline, Adrift by Kay Bratt
Book 6: Moonlight on the Lido Deck by Violet Howe

Also by Violet Howe

Tales Behind the Veils

Diary of a Single Wedding Planner

Diary of a Wedding Planner in Love

Diary of an Engaged Wedding Planner

Maggie

The Cedar Creek Collection

Cedar Creek Mysteries:

The Ghost in the Curve

The Glow in the Woods

The Phantom in the Footlights

Cedar Creek Families:

Building Fences

Crossing Paths

Cedar Creek Suspense:

Whiskey Flight

Bounty Flight

Fallen Bloodlines

Vampire Born

(Continued on next page)

Soul Sisters at Cedar Mountain Lodge

Christmas Sisters

Christmas Hope

Christmas Peace

Christmas Secret

Visit www.violethowe.com to subscribe to Violet's monthly newsletter.

Acknowledgments

First and foremost, thank you to my fellow Sail Away Series authors for being my travel mates on this journey.

Thank you to Melissa for being such a wonderful accountability partner and for giving me unwavering support and encouragement. I'm so happy you are part of my author tribe!

A huge thanks to Tammy for talking me off the ledge and being there when I needed a compassionate leader and a friend.

Thanks to Teresa for dropping everything and traveling with me on this ship.

Thanks to John for being a fabulous cruise partner and for being willing to go on a cruise just for research purposes. And for your support through the last two weeks of this process.

Thanks to Delia and Dan for the Crumbl runs and the support and understanding. So thankful for y'all!

About the Author

Violet Howe lives in Florida with her husband and their adorable but spoiled dogs. When she's not writing, Violet is usually watching movies, reading, or planning her next travel adventure. She believes in happily ever afters, love conquering all, humor being essential to life, and pizza being a necessity.

Newsletter
Visit www.violethowe.com to subscribe and be the first to know about Violet's new releases, giveaways, sales, and appearances.
Facebook Group
You can also find out about joining Violet's Facebook Reader Group, the Ultra Violets.

Made in the USA
Monee, IL
02 April 2023